ROUGH PATCH

SCREAMING DEMONS MC
BOOK FIVE

SUMMER COOPER

SIENNA CHANCE

LOVY BOOKS

ess than a year ago, Fiona Strong was a genius. Since then... she'd married, gotten pregnant, lost her father, taken over the Screaming Demons motorcycle club and its various enterprises and empire, and lost every damned brain cell she'd ever owned. All because of her husband, Grier Owen.

Her office—once her father's—was frilly and girlie and white and Hamilton couldn't have looked more out of place. She slammed the folder closed and stared at him as he sat across the desk in a chair too small and fragile for a man his size. "Are you sure?"

He nodded. His short hair catching the light thanks to the gel he loved so much and his face grim, normal, but grim. "Yeah. Dave was FBI. His wife isn't even his wife. She's an agent too and the kids... maybe junior agents?" It was as close to a smile as Fiona had ever seen from him. Hamilton, her best friend, knew everything about her, and she knew everything about him. From his clenched fists and burning eyes, the only thing keeping him in his chair and rather than finding Grier and committing a murder, was her, their friendship and his respect for the fact killing Grier would take an order from her. Normally Hamilton was more the kind of guy who believed it was easier to ask forgiveness than permission. Thank God there was nothing normal about this.

Well, fuck. "Dave's gone now, so I suppose we need to thank whoever rid us of that particular problem." Although, no telling how much intel he'd fed all his agent friends, how much he knew about the whole operation. "Who are we thanking, Ham?"

She'd put him on this as soon as she saw the picture of Grier handing a mysterious envelope to Dave, even before she'd gone to Ralph's to verify the authenticity of the picture. And while it broke her heart to do it, Grier had left her no choice. Wouldn't tell her anything.

"I don't know yet." His tone said he had an opinion he just wasn't sharing with her. And that was very much not like him at all. If he knew for sure, though, he would have led with it.

Fiona stared at Hamilton, his short military haircut,

his stormy gray eyes, the build that would have scared any sensible man. Her best friend. "Do you trust Grier?"

His blank expression gave away nothing. "If you trust him, I trust him."

She needed his truth right now, not the auto-agreement he'd always given Max. "That isn't what I mean. Do *you* trust Grier?" His silence spoke volumes, and the ticking clock on the bookshelf in the corner counted the seconds she waited for an answer that wasn't coming. "Never mind."

There were a thousand reasons that she shouldn't trust Grier, shouldn't even want to, but to believe he'd gone to the FBI, to consider it, hurt. Physically.

"Fiona, what do you want to do?" Hamilton's stare burned into her, as if he was trying to see inside her mind, her empty, without a clue how to fix this mind.

She picked up the second folder. "This is all the PI could find?"

"Just some background history, a couple of pictures from social media. Not even a birth certificate." He shrugged as if the past didn't matter near as much as the present they were dealing with right now.

"I saw his birth certificate the day we got married."

"Could have been a fake."

Fiona hadn't considered that. If Grier was FBI, they could have faked his documents. She opened the folder in her hand. For containing information so important to the club, it weighed nothing.

She read the summary page. "Nothing here." She skimmed a few paragraphs down then looked away from the page and out the window. The sun was bright even through the sheer window shade. The whir of the fan overhead drowned out birds she knew would be chirping. And she was tired. So damned tired of all of this. "Hamilton, he was sixteen when he came here and he's been with us ever since except when he left with Kye. No way would he have gone to the feds." He might not have loved Max, but he respected him, had his hands in enough of Max's business that he would be counted equally as guilty. She tried to think of specific laws he'd broken, things that, if he was some undercover whatever, would end that particular career. Damned if she'd ever seen him get his hands dirty, though until he'd gone, she'd been shielded from the dark side of the business. "Do you remember when Grier showed up here?"

"It was a dark and stormy night…" Grier spoke from the doorway, and Fiona spun her chair to look at him.

Woah. All in black, from his leather jacket to his jeans and t-shirt, Grier was beautiful. Tan and beautiful. Tall, tan, and… oh, enough already. He could have worn a brown paper bag and been striking. Of course, that wouldn't save him—even she wouldn't be able to save him—if he was a rat or a plant from the FBI.

He pushed off the wall and strode in to plunk down in the chair next to Hamilton. "Rent." The brown paper envelope landed on her desk and the flap spilled open. A few twenties slid toward the edge.

Hamilton stood. "I'll be in the garage if you need me." He leaned down and dropped a hand to Grier's shoulder. "She better not need me." He gave a squeeze that inspired a wince from Grier before he walked out. It was going to take a while before Hamilton got into the forgive and forget portion of the program with Grier. Especially in light of this new information.

"Grier…" She needed a plan. Something better than the friends close, enemies closer thing her father employed. If Grier was FBI or was hiding some other deep dark secret, she didn't have time to flush it out of him. She needed to know now. "Do you want to come for dinner tonight?"

This invitation had nothing to do with how much the pathetic parts of her missed him. She didn't give two damns about them. This was about protecting the club, its business, and all the men who'd been loyal to her father.

His eyebrows lifted and he smiled. "Yeah."

He held her gaze until she had to look away, couldn't stand looking anymore. "Nothing special, just… dinner."

"I won't pack a toothbrush."

Enemies closer. "I might have a spare if you need it."

And whether or not it was a result of pregnancy hormones or the man himself, a part of her hoped he would need it.

* * *

DINNER WITH FIONA. He hadn't had a moment's peace since she'd made the invitation. Nor a clear thought. He missed her. He wanted her. But he'd let her down. Repeatedly. Sent her straight into that asshat's trap, then failed to find Tyler Sedotal when she'd had to shoot him. And, he'd left her to deal with the aftermath all on her own. Of course, she hadn't given him much choice. She'd taken a room at the clubhouse and made it clear he wasn't invited in.

Each thought chased another until they wrapped around the pile of lies he'd created. Lies he wanted to explain but couldn't. Yet. Not until he caught Sedotal, at least. Then he would come clean. He would tell her all of it. And face whatever the consequences.

He stood on the front porch and squeezed the stems of the paper-wrapped flowers in his left hand then relaxed so they lived long enough to make it inside the house. He knocked on the door. Of his own house. And waited.

Every second he stood out there was worth it. When

she swung the door open, his breath whooshed out. Holy shit. A negligee. Sheer. Nipples. He could only think in single words. His dick throbbed, sprang to life, and he thrust the flowers out in front of him. "Here."

She tugged him inside by the collar of his shirt and tossed the bouquet on the table as she pressed her lips against his, forced her tongue in his mouth, and curled her leg around his hip.

His arms wrapped around her waist, and he kicked the door shut behind him. The neighbors didn't need to see what was about to happen. Although, if he had his way, they'd probably hear it. He walked her backward to the sofa, never breaking the kiss.

She moaned into his mouth as he cupped her ass then slid his hand lower until he could feel the wet heat of her pussy. She shifted her hips to meet his fingers, and his eyelids fluttered shut. Oh, God. Nothing in the world felt as good and as right as Fiona. She ground against his fingers, whimpered, and groaned, then tore her mouth away from his and attacked his belt and button-fly. When she wrapped her hand around his cock, his breath halted.

She turned and bent over, bracing herself against the back of the sofa. A thin string of lace peeked from between her ass cheeks and she jerked it to the side, holding it away. "Fuck me, Grier."

And though he loved hearing it, he wouldn't make her ask twice. He shoved down his jeans, and his dick sprang free, ready to push inside of her. When he paused, wondered if it was safe for the baby, she reached for his dick, positioned it against her pussy then slid until she had every inch. Oh, God. This was and would always be home.

* * *

THE SECOND TIME, they'd made it as far as the stairs. Grier hadn't even managed to say *hello* or *thank you* or *I love you* before she'd pushed him down and climbed on top. She'd ridden him, pounding her hips against his until she arched her back and cried out his name over and over. Then she'd collapsed against him, and he'd carried her to bed.

Now she had her head on his shoulder, and he brushed his hand over her hair. He couldn't stop touching her, couldn't stop smiling, either. "I think we should have dinner every night."

She swirled a finger around his nipple then lifted her head for a quick kiss. "You think so?" Her smile didn't reach her eyes, and Grier's gut clenched. This wasn't the look of a satisfied woman who'd just spent the last couple of hours rocking her husband's world onto its side. This was an angry woman.

She sat up and pulled on a robe before she stood and walked to the attached bathroom. Grier folded his hands behind his head and waited. After a few minutes, she came out with a toothbrush in her mouth. "I think we should move back in here. Together, I mean."

Grier couldn't play this game with her right now. Not with Sedotal still on the loose and the FBI breathing down his neck so close they probably knew every scratch on his back from her nails. Dave dying hadn't been good for Grier on any front.

"I thought you didn't want to stay here." She was safer at the club where one of the guys was always around to protect her while he was off looking for Sedotal.

She'd walked back into the bathroom but poked her head around the corner. "I miss my house. And I miss sleeping in a place that doesn't smell like stale beer and pot." She came out of the bathroom and sat beside him on the bed. "And I miss my husband." Nice to hear, but the lie darkened her eyes.

Being around her right now was dangerous for her. He couldn't risk her life or the baby's. But damned if he wanted to be anywhere else than in her house and in her bed. He wanted to be the man in her life, protecting her and their baby. He only wished she wanted it too, and her eyes said she didn't.

She ran a manicured nail along his thigh where it

poked out from beneath the sheet. Thinking became ever more difficult as she inched toward his dick. In the interest of forming actual words, he covered her roving hand with his and tugged until she moved half on top of him with only the sheet and the thin layer of her robe between him and heaven. "If you want to come home…"

She kissed his nipple. "I want *us* to come home." Her breathy voice along with her fingers stroking him through the blanket made refusal an impossibility. "But I need to know everything so I can protect myself."

When the words finally broke through the haze in his head, his hard-on died a sad and pathetic little death. Goddammit. She didn't give a shit about him coming home. She was after answers. Answers he couldn't give.

He slid out of bed on the other side. "Jesus, Fiona. You could've just asked me if you wanted to know about the picture." His anger was unreasonable. Maybe even unwarranted but hurt coursed through him. She'd used her body. Thought he'd be too blinded by desire to resist telling her everything she wanted to know. "Could have saved yourself all the fucking and faking."

Her tone hardened. "Of course I want to know about the picture. I want to know why my husband is handing over an envelope of God knows what to the fucking FBI." She whirled to face him as he zipped his jeans. "And I fucked you because I wanted to. Because you're my husband, and I wanted *you.*" Her eyes flashed and she punched her hands onto her hips.

It was a pretty convincing show of indignance, and if he'd bought it, he might have felt a tiny bit of guilt. "Bullshit. You fucked me because you thought you're so in my head that if you used your body, I would just lie back and tell you the things that could get you killed."

"And you're so noble you would've said no? So damned self-righteous you would have tucked your dick and walked away rather than risk my life… as if you give one shit about me."

He stalked out the bedroom and downstairs before he said something he couldn't take back or worse told her everything.

"Yeah, run away again. It's what you do, isn't it?" She taunted him from the top of the steps then raced down to grab his shoulder and spin him around. "I don't need you to protect me. I'm a big girl."

Well, this damned sure wasn't doing either of them any good. He tamped down his anger and stared at her. "You are?" He kept his tone soft.

She squinted. "Yeah."

"A big, tough girl." He slipped his arm around her waist and pulled her in then lowered his head to slide a line of kisses along her jaw. If she could use sex, maybe he could too. With his free hand, he loosened the belt to her robe and cupped her breast. As he ran his thumb over her nipple, she gripped his shoulders.

"What are you doing?"

He smiled. "If you don't know, I must be doing it wrong." He took the nipple in his mouth and swirled his tongue until she whimpered and clung to him.

"This isn't going to work." But she lined her hips up with his.

"Feels like it's working." He lowered his hand and dragged it along her clit, seeking out her warm wet pussy. Just a tease would do for now, something to take her mind off the issue he couldn't yet address. He slid a finger inside her, and she closed her eyes. "Oh yeah. Definitely working." As his fingers pumped in and out of her, she bent her knees, riding his hand and moaning until his dick throbbed with need. He pulled away. "You want some more?"

Her eyes fluttered shut, and her knees buckled. He wanted her like he'd never wanted anything before in his life. He swept her up, waited for her to hang on. But her arms went limp at her sides and her head lolled. He moved her to the couch, laid her down. "Fiona?" She didn't answer. Didn't even move. His heart stopped as he tangled his fingers through her hair and forced her face toward his. Her eyes were closed but her breath puffed out in short gasps. She'd passed out and Grier didn't know much, but he knew that wasn't normal. He reached for his phone.

Fear made his hands shake as he dialed. Before the voice asked him his emergency, "My wife collapsed." He rattled off the address. "You have to hurry." If something happened to Fiona because of him…

2

For hell's sake. This was ridiculous. She was dehydrated, not dying, and the number of nurses and random people in and out of her room who weren't Grier did nothing to help her disposition. A bag of clear liquid connected by a tube to her arm dripped soundlessly, but the heart monitor attached to her chest more than made up for it. A tight set of bands wrapped around her stomach and another machine at her side spit paper with two sets of wiggling lines. And she was hungry. Starving, actually.

And there were a thousand reasons she needed to get out of this bed and back to work. She pushed the button to call the nurse.

A woman in scrubs the color of Pepto Bismol breezed in. "What can I do for you?" Her attitude matched her clothes—too bright.

"Where's my husband?"

"I believe he's down in registration. I'm sure he'll be back soon." She checked the I.V. bag then pulled the paper from the other machine and stared at it. "Baby's heartbeat is strong."

Of course it was. Half-Fiona, half-Grier. This kid would probably be invincible. "When can I go home?" She just wanted to sink into her own bed and sleep the rest of the night—correction: day—away.

"In a couple of hours. We want to get this bag of fluid in and the doctor wants an ultrasound before you go." She scribbled something on the paper then dropped it back into the slot where it automatically folded into neat little rectangles. "And we need to get someone in to talk nutrition and rest with you."

Fiona glared. A couple of hours were probably two more than she could spare to lie in a bed and do nothing. And the last thing she needed was someone telling her how to live. She had secrets to uncover, a mystery to solve. And she couldn't very go full Nancy Drew when the only clothes she had on were a gown that tied in the back and a pair of fuzzy socks with those little no-slip lines on the bottom.

But an ultrasound. A picture of her baby. It wouldn't take a lot of convincing to get her to stick around for that. She laid back against the pillow and stared at the ceiling. By the time she'd counted the ceiling tiles—

seventy-two—Grier returned, his face haggard and his eyes rimmed in red.

"Hey." He stood at the side of the bed, hands gripping the rail so hard his knuckles were white.

"Hey." Maybe one day they'd get better at small talk. Today wasn't that day. "Did you get the papers all filled out?"

He nodded. "I forgot your middle name. So I put down Henrietta. I hope you don't mind." His half-smile and the way he ducked his head and looked at her from beneath those damned long lashes made her heart skitter and since she was still hooked to the monitor, he knew it.

"Henrietta's fine. Thank you." The silence stretched between them. "The nurse said they want to do an ultrasound." He nodded, and she watched his face. Either he felt guilty, or he was as scared as she was. Maybe a little of both. "Grier…"

"I'm so sorry, Fiona."

Guilt. "It's not your fault."

He brought his hand up to scrub over his face and flip his hair to one side. His chest heaved. "I knew Dave was FBI." He fumbled with the rail, she guessed trying to lower it, but instead he ended up jerking it and pulling the wheeled bed a few inches to her left. "Goddammit."

His hand was warm when she rested hers on top. "There's a release." The nurse had lowered the rail to adjust the bands around her belly, and she'd reached below the mattress. Fiona waited while he found it. This was one of the single most important conversations in her life. Damned if she'd ruin it by rushing him. He breathed out slowly, and sat beside her, took her hand in his, and closed his eyes.

"I'm not a spy or a traitor. I was paying Dave for information."

Fiona didn't draw away or speak or do more than let him hold her hand and remain silent because she didn't know what to say yet.

"I met him in a bar one night a long time ago." He sighed. "I didn't know then, but after a while, he tried to get me to turn on your dad. I went to Max, and I told him the FBI was sniffing around him. This was before all the Kye and Eliana stuff."

Fiona couldn't tell if he was lying. Grier didn't have a single tell and he kept his eyes pointed right at hers. If she had to guess, she would have said he was probably telling the truth, but if Max had known about the FBI investigating him, she couldn't imagine him letting it happen. Still, she remained silent.

"At the time, we were ass deep in drugs and guns and stolen cars and merchandise. Max couldn't afford jail. So, he met with Dave, paid him a shitload of money to back off. And Max started going legit, a little bit at a time. And all the while, Dave was milking the club for more money."

The story made no sense. Max would never have submitted to an extortionist. "Grier…"

"I know. I thought Max would have him killed. I did. But I paid Dave every month for Max." He chuckled a little. "And then Max turned those tables. He had videos of Dave taking payments every month. Recordings of Dave feeding me information. All of a sudden, we had a man on the inside of the FBI." He looked down. "The picture of me and Dave is me paying him for information. He wired the truck with video which would feed to a computer *somewhere,* and we'd know who was stealing our shipments."

Fiona watched him. If it was a lie, it was a damned good one. Nothing she could verify either. "But he died before we got the information."

"Yeah. And Dave wasn't stupid. He's been your dad's truck driver for ten years." He shook his head and the lines in his beautiful face deepened. "And I don't know who has that computer or what's on it. So when I'm gone, I'm either out looking for that bastard Sedotal or I'm trying to get information on Dave and that fucking computer."

"Why didn't you just tell me?" She might have been able to help.

He brushed her bangs off her forehead, and her heart

sped up again. Damned machine. "I'm a traitor, Fiona, remember? And our relationship isn't exactly a fairy tale."

"This was club stuff. You should've told me."

He nodded and turned his gaze away. "I wanted to prove to you that I'm… in with the club again. I wanted you to trust me." He shook his head. "And then it all got away from me. Now I don't know who has the computer. If it's at the FBI… I can tell them it was me… all me. I can keep the club safe. If anyone else has it, they'll know to come to me and only me. I didn't want this to… touch you until I could fix it, until I could show you I would protect you."

This was a lot to digest. "So we're looking for a video that may or may not make you look guilty of… something." She didn't want to even contemplate. "An asshole that tried to…" Okay. She still couldn't say that word. She shook her head instead. "And someone inside the club and whoever they're telling our business to. Do I have that right?"

Grier nodded. Stared at her with eyes he couldn't have hidden a lie behind. At least, she didn't think so. "I wouldn't sell out the club, Fiona. I wouldn't do anything to hurt you or the baby or the club."

And God she wanted to believe him, wanted him to be the loyal guy he said. but the FBI? And Max knew and never said? Even to her? Or Hamilton. This wasn't just Max's business. It was club business. And the club should've been informed. If it was even true.

She didn't answer with more than a nod because her head was too full, and a woman wheeled yet another machine into the room. This was too much to think about with a tech lifting her ugly gown, removing the bands attached to monitor two and squirting gel on her belly. Grier sat beside Fiona still but turned to see the screen where a rounded bottom triangle of black and murky white changed dimension with every swipe of the flat-edged scope.

"All right. There… is your baby." The woman used her free hand to point out a white blob in the center of the black. A beautiful white blob. But this time, she could see a face… kind of. Holes where the eyes should've been, a head too big for the body, and a perfect little nose and mouth.

She glanced at Grier, saw his teary smile, and her own eyes brimmed. "Can you see?"

He nodded and swallowed hard, even squeezed her hand as the tech pushed some buttons on the machine and moved the scope again. The baby, from another view, appeared on the screen, and nothing in the world mattered more to Fiona than her little family and keeping it together.

* * *

GRIER KEPT his arm around Fiona as if he moved it, she would collapse. For all he knew, she might have. Between being sick and everything he'd laid on her, she'd been through a lot in the last twenty-four hours. Another collapse wouldn't have been unwarranted. And it would have been his fault. Again.

Her lingerie still draped on the stair rail and the couch was still cock-eyed from the ambulance guys pushing it out of the way to make room for the stretcher. He gave it a shove with his hip, and Fiona laughed as it slid a foot too far.

"Just leave it." She tried to shrug him away as he guided her to the stairs. "I'm hungry."

"I'll make you something. Or I'll order something, but you need to be in bed."

She narrowed her eyes. "Doctor said I was fine. Just to drink a lot of water. He didn't say anything about bed."

No, he hadn't, but no way were they taking any more chances. He grinned. "I think you might be looking at this all wrong." He turned her so her chest pressed against his then he swung her into his arms and carried her upstairs before he spoke again. "Any woman who has my baby is entitled to the royal treatment. That means no cooking, no cleaning, breakfast lunch and dinner in bed, round trip service to and from the bathroom, and so much more that I'm sure will come up in the next few days." And as much as he wanted to kiss her, he set her in the middle of the bed instead. This hands-to-himself thing was going to be a lot tougher than he thought. "You earned yourself an all-access, twenty-four-seven personal valet."

Fiona pursed her lips and shucked the gown she'd worn home from the hospital. Grier's tongue grew thick and his heart rate sped toward the danger zone.

"Thank you, but no thank you. I am capable of going into the office, seeing to my own meals, and if you so much as try to carry me to the bathroom, I'm probably going to kill you in your sleep."

"Which I'll be doing on that pillow, right there." He pointed to the left side of the bed—closest to the door in case of intruders, which in light of all recent events didn't seem as scary as it sounded. "Now, let's get you into some comfy jammies and snuggled into bed."

She looked him up and down, her gaze leaving a path of fire everywhere it touched, and he had to remind himself that she had a baby inside of her that probably didn't need Daddy's dick upsetting everything in there. But when she knee-walked to the end of the bed and tugged him by the collar, he didn't resist. "The only way I'm staying in bed for even one day is if you're in it with me." She rolled them with a ridiculous amount of strength for someone so small then kissed him softly. "And we need to talk."

They did. And they would. But not now, not when she'd just come from the hospital. Not when she kissed her way from his mouth to his jaw to his ear. Not when she threw her thigh over his cock and glided it back and forth.

"Talk is way over-rated." He closed his eyes and enjoyed the feel of her against him, the brush of her fingers under his shirt as she reached for his zipper.

With her mouth against his ear, her warm breath heated him from lobe to gut. Her words took care of the rest. "I want you to put your dick in my mouth."

Oh, God, yes.

But if she… if he… then the baby… no.

He pulled away and sat up. Fiona grunted out a frustrated sigh and threw herself against the pillow. "What the hell?"

The images in his head made his stomach churn so he closed his eyes and shook his head. "I don't…"

"Don't what? Want me?"

And he would have been fine if her voice hadn't broken and if she hadn't sniffed. Now he'd hurt her. "No. That's not it at all. I want you. Make no mistake. I. Want. You." And looking at her did nothing to help that particular affliction. "I just don't want…" It sounded stupid. Certainly pregnant women could have sex. Her doctor had said so both at the office appointment and again that morning before they'd left the hospital. But

Grier couldn't wrap his head around the baby digesting… ick. New thought.

"Then what's the problem?"

"Fiona…" His skin burned again for an entirely different reason. Embarrassment. Shame. Ridiculousness.

"The doctor said sex is fine and it won't hurt the baby."

Times like this, he wished he had a dad to talk to about this kind of thing. He couldn't imagine broaching this subject with anyone else. "Don't you think we should talk about the FBI thing?"

"We will. In depth. Later. Right now, I want to talk about this."

She had a determined glow in her eyes, and he had to look away. And no damned way were they discussing his little hang-up. Nine months wasn't that long to go without sliding his dick into her, without feeling her mouth on his skin, without… Fiona. Fuck. He'd be lucky to last nine minutes. He scooted a few more inches away.

"You just got out of the hospital. Don't you think we should take it easy?" He said a silent prayer she would let it go, just take his totally reasonable explanation, and drop this whole subject.

"I'm trying to make it easy." She sat up long enough to pull him down beside her again. Her lips were firm and her tongue determined, but he kept his mouth closed. She jerked back and rolled away. "Goddammit, Grier."

And he should have said something, soothed whatever thoughts—misguided and wrong as they were—from her mind, but he couldn't explain. Didn't even know how to put words to his fucked-up thoughts. He slid one arm under her head and the other around her waist then pulled her back against him.

"What are you doing?" But she didn't wiggle away or push him to his own side of the bed. She actually moved closer.

"I want to take a middle of the day nap with my wife, and I want to hold her while I sleep." When she sat up to adjust his arm under her head then laid down again, he smiled. "And don't worry about your snoring. It won't bother me at all."

She kissed the inside of his wrist. "Then I won't let yours bother me."

Even if it was only for this one minute or for the hour or so he planned to nap, it would be one of those perfect memories he etched into his mind that would get him through after he lost her.

3

iona stretched her arms over her head and sat up. The blanket rustled and fell to her lap. The fan whirred overhead, and the evening sunlight left a glow of orange on the white carpet in her room. Her bed, in the center of the room, creaked and shifted as she moved back into her place beside him.

They'd been through so much already. A forced marriage. Even if it was her idea, she'd forced him into it and he'd gone along… she'd yet to figure out why. Then Sedotal had tried to rape her. Even tried to kill her. Then Grier. Then the picture of Grier with the FBI and his hospital confessions. She'd always known marriage wasn't supposed to be easy, but come on. Was it really supposed to be like this?

Grier stirred but didn't wake, and she watched him for a minute. The twitch of his eyelids and his frown said this was not a pleasant dream he was having. His arm flexed, and she smoothed a gentle hand over his chest. He calmed and rolled toward her. When his eyes opened, he smiled. "Hi."

"Hi." After everything they'd done, everything they'd been through and knew about one another, Fiona was shy. She couldn't look at him. "Did you sleep well?"

"Yeah." His arms curled around her just a little tighter, and as much as she didn't want to melt into him, her body went pliable and soft. They had so many things to talk about, so much to straighten out, but more she wanted to bask in this moment, let him hold her and pretend everything in the world wasn't against them.

Her stomach grumbled, and she covered it with her hand. "I think the kid is hungry."

He sat up straight, like he had a springboard attached to his back. "I'll get us something." He climbed out of bed and marched out of the room—a man on a mission. And if he seriously thought he was going to find much in her fridge, he was headed down a long, disappointing road.

She pulled the landline phone—an old rotary that had come with the place—off her bedside table and a menu from the drawer. The diner at the end of the block delivered and she could get "homemade" meals brought right to her door.

"We need to grocery shop." Grier stood in the doorway, hands in his pockets, chest still bare. Good enough to eat.

"How about some delivery from Cal's Café?" She held up the menu. "They have roast beef, burgers, spaghetti, all the best stuff." Her mouth watered at the thought of chili-cheese fries.

"If that's what you want." He smiled slowly, and if she didn't know him, she would think him timid, but he had a glimmer in his eyes, a hunger that certainly had nothing to do with food.

Maybe food could wait just a little longer. She let the blanket slip a few inches toward her waist then patted the side of the bed where he'd slept. "Come here." She took in his every step—the long legs, bare toes, smooth, broad chest—as he closed the distance between them.

Instead of sitting behind her, he sat in front, one leg dangling off the bed and the other tucked under him— too far to touch without leaning and stretching. Was he trying to tell her something? The blanket fell a bit lower, and true to plan, his gaze rested on the curve of her breast.

He cleared his throat and took the menu. "What are you getting?"

She shuffled across the bed to sit beside him, angled her body so her nipple rubbed against his biceps. More than she wanted food, she wanted Grier. She kissed his shoulder and let her hand fall into his lap. His body stiffened, and not in the good way. "What's the problem, Grier?"

"No problem." The crack in his voice said otherwise.

"Horny, naked wife wants husband who isn't interested. It's what I call a problem." She moved back to the head of the bed. If she wasn't getting a good fuck, she'd settle for a good pout.

"Fiona, you just collapsed, okay? Maybe you should take it easy." Great. Now he sounded like Max. At the thought of her father, her heart pinged with sadness and the mood died. Grier scooted closer and held out a hand. And because she was weak for him, she took it and let his thumb stroking her palm hypnotize her into smiling.

"Fine. But I'm not always going to take no for an answer."

He tangled his free hand in her hair and leaned in for a kiss that rocked her from shoulder blade to shin bone. When he pulled back, he had that glint in his eyes, the one full of promises and naughty pleasures. He nuzzled her cheek with his nose then whispered, "You will until I say so."

Warmth fluttered through her. She liked Grier in control. She'd always been the one in charge—at the club, in her personal life—but it felt good to surrender to him. Too good. "I will until I'm tired of taking no for an answer."

He smiled as if he knew something she didn't, then stood. "Let's order dinner." He snatched the menu and read. "And after we eat, we'll talk."

"About all of it."

"About most of it. I'll tell you as much as I can."

Which meant he would tell her nothing, but it was the best she was going to get for now, so she settled against the headboard and waited.

* * *

GRIER SUCKED the last of the chili from her fingers. "Tastes better this way." He held her hand a minute longer then stood to gather the trash and take it downstairs. When he returned and stood leaning against the doorframe, still bare-chested and tousled, she smiled and crooked the finger still tingling from being inside his mouth.

"Come here."

She'd dressed in a pair of running shorts and a t-shirt she was fully prepared to strip off with just the slightest nod from him. A nod that didn't seem likely since he hadn't moved from the doorway.

"I thought you wanted to talk." His voice was thick as she let her hand glide over her thigh to the edge of her shorts. Yes, she wanted to talk. She wanted all the details, but she wouldn't get them while his stubborn ass remained clear-headed. She needed his mind clouded by desire, his body throbbing for her. Plus, she was still horny. This pregnancy thing was the best aphrodisiac.

"Oh, I do want to talk." But she slipped her fingers inside her shorts, touched her already pulsating clit. With her free hand, she shoved the t-shirt up and cupped her breast, watching him. "But I need this first."

"Take your shorts off." His voice, husky and demanding, didn't break this time as he moved toward the bed. When he stood over her, he repeated his command. "Take your shorts off." He leaned down to suck her exposed nipple into his mouth, teasing her with his tongue until she couldn't think of anything more than Grier. She arched her back and continued to work her swollen pussy.

"I will if you will." She punctuated the words with breaths between.

"You will because I said so." He pulled away and stood, eyes dark, dick bulging behind the fly of his pants. And she'd never seen anything hotter, never wanted anyone or anything more in her life than she wanted Grier. She pushed her shorts down and kicked them away then stripped off her shirt. "Now lie down."

Fiona scooted to the center of the bed and waited. His gaze burned over her skin, and her body flamed for him, for Grier. He slid onto the bed beside her and feathered his finger down her throat to the valley between her breasts over her stomach to her pubic bone. His kisses followed the same trail. And her breath caught and held in her throat until she released it in a long sigh when his mouth closed over her clit.

Nothing in the world, except maybe having him inside her, felt so exquisite. She lifted her hips, and he drew away. "Lie still."

No way. Her body needed to move, needed him closer, needed her husband inside her. He lowered his head and kissed the inside of her thigh. "Grier." She curled her fingers in his hair and he removed her hand, sucking each finger into his mouth before laying it beside her and kissing her thigh again, his mouth so close to where she wanted, needed him.

"Don't make me tell you again." He teased her with the tip of his tongue and a finger against the opening to her pussy, so close but not close enough. She lifted her hips, urging him to ease the pressure building inside of her. He lifted his head. "Fiona."

"Please, Grier. Please." She fluttered her fingers against the blanket then brought them to her nipples, pinching and tweaking while he watched. If there was a penalty for touching herself, he didn't mention, only watched her for a minute before lowering his head again.

Ecstasy fired through her cells. Nothing mattered but Grier's mouth on her, his fingers curling in and out as she strained closer to the edge. When she cried out and her body shuddered, he lapped at her until she lay trembling against the aftershocks.

Oh, God. This man.

He moved beside her and drew her against him. When she fumbled with his waistband, he brought her hand to his mouth and kissed the knuckles. "Do you want to talk now?"

No. She didn't. She wanted to fuck her husband. She wanted his cock inside of her. She wanted…

And she would wait.

* * *

GRIER'S BREATH came in uneven gusts. There was nothing he liked more than seeing Fiona spread before him, eager for his touch, for his mouth, for his everything, but they needed to talk, and he needed her calm, her full attention on his words.

And he needed his head clear, not fogged by desire or lust or whatever the hell had him standing in the bathroom, dick in his hand. He stroked slowly, his eyes closed, remembering the taste of her, the way she'd writhed under his mouth when she came, the little squeals and whimpers of pleasure.

His hand tightened around his cock, and he used his finger to caress the sweet spot just under the head, the way Fiona used her tongue when she sucked him off. Oh, God. Fiona.

He imagined her bent in front of him, pussy glistening, hands guiding him into her, body pounding against his, taking every inch of his cock… Oh, God.

The door opened and his eyes snapped open as she knelt in front of him, took him into her mouth and sucked, cupping his balls with one hand, and using the other to stroke the base in rhythm with her mouth.

"Fuck."

Her head bobbed, and he couldn't hold back anymore. His body shook with the power of the orgasm as her mouth milked every last drop. Had the wall not been behind him and Fiona in front, he would certainly have collapsed. Instead, he worked to catch his breath as Fiona glared up at him.

"You'd rather jerk off in the bathroom than fuck me? Nice." She stood and turned away from him, though he could still see her in the mirror, see the hurt in her eyes.

Shit. This was a conversation he didn't want and couldn't have. Not with her. Not with anyone until he had some time to Google. He wrapped his arms around her from behind and kissed her neck. "There is nothing in this world I would rather do than fuck you."

"Really?" His dick was still hanging out and his jeans were bunched around his ankles. The evidence didn't roll in his favor, and she knew it.

He sighed and let go long enough to yank up his pants before settling against her again. "Yes, really." No time for the internet, he spun her to face him. "I don't want the kid to… our kid is in there." He wagged a finger toward her waist. "And if I'm…" He couldn't say it. "Don't you want to know about Dave and the FBI?"

"Later. Right now I want to know why I found my husband standing in the bathroom taking matters into his own hands when I am one room away ready and willing to fuck him cross-eyed. Then we can chat about the FBI."

Well, didn't she just have a way with words.

He grinned. "Am I the cross-eyed one in this little scenario, or are you?"

She whirled and gave him a little shove. "Don't try to charm me, Grier. I want to know why you're in here instead of out there in bed with me."

He pulled the door open and walked through. "Well, I don't want to talk about that." Because it sounded stupid. Made him sound stupid.

She followed on his heels. "Tough. I do."

Dammit. Where the hell was his shirt? Not on the chair or the floor or under the bed. And goddammit, he needed a shirt. Couldn't stand in a room with half-naked Fiona, bare-chested and have a conversation like this one or any other right now.

She crossed her arms. "Grier."

The force in her tone made him look at her. It had nothing to do with how badly he wanted to look at her. He threw up his hands then crossed his arms. One way or the other they would be having the conversation at some point. Nothing to do but get it out of the way. "I don't want the kid to… come out with a dent in its head."

"What?" To her credit, she didn't outright laugh, only smirked. "Grier, the doctor said sex will *not* hurt the baby."

He nodded, heat burning its way from his toes to his ears. "I know. I was there."

"And the baby is way up here." She pointed to a spot on her abdomen. "You're impressive, but…" She shrugged. Then chuckled. "The baby's head will be just fine." Now his ego joined his pride in aching. He couldn't look at her laughing at him. Not even when she slid her body against his and dropped a shoulder to try to force him to see her. "I like that you care though." She laid her head over his heart. "I like it a lot."

She sniffed and a bead of water rolled down to his stomach. She was crying.

"Hey." He tilted her chin up and brushed away another as it fell over her lashes. "I'm sorry." He didn't know what else to say.

"Fucking hormones. One minute I'm ready to ravish your body, the next I could tear your throat out, and now I'm bawling like you stole my Barbie doll." She shook her head. "What is wrong with me?"

He didn't laugh, couldn't, because she might have killed him, but mostly because he wanted to soothe her. "We're having a baby." And this time, the words meant something, had him thinking of the kind of father he would be, the kind who read bedtime stories, and chased away monsters from under the bed, and loved his family more than anything else in the world. He would be the father he'd never had.

4

Fiona crunched a mouthful of ice and stared at Hamilton. "He said Dave was feeding information to him about another club. The Omens. When Dad stepped out of the drug trade"—not completely out—"they took over. Started selling some bad shit."

Hamilton shrugged. "Never heard of them." He leaned back, putting his chair on its back two legs, and Fiona fought another wave of nausea. Morning sickness was not her friend. She bit into another cube of ice. Hamilton shoveled in another mouthful of runny eggs. "I would think your old man would have shared that kind of information with all of us, not just Grier."

"He said Dad had him out looking for the leader, trying to become one of them."

Okay. Even to Fiona, it sounded far-fetched. Especially that her dad didn't tell anyone else in the club, but she wanted, more than anything to believe in Grier.

"And he never found him?" Hamilton cocked his head with a meaningful look, with his she- was-such-a-dumbass look.

She shook her head, trying to save a bit of dignity and prove she wasn't as ridiculous as he thought. "The whole bit with Kye and his woman happened." She remembered those days vividly. Her dad had ended up shot. Kye and Eliana on the run. Grier gone without a word. Missing shipments. Stolen goods and their customers bolting like God himself had come calling. Money tight enough it looked bad for the club until Max figured out how to fix it. Not that he'd ever explained how he'd managed to turn it all around.

Her stomach churned, and she closed her eyes, breathing in and out slowly, hoping to settle her rebellious body into submission. "You okay, Fi? You're looking a little green."

She swallowed a mouthful of saliva and took another deep breath. "This kid might be trying to kill me."

"Anything I can do?" He set his fork down and braced both hands on the edge of the table as if he would throw it out of the way to get to her if she needed.

The nausea passed, and she nodded. "Yeah. You can find out what about his story is true. Keep someone on him all the time." She pushed her hair back, every bit the traitor she felt. Traitor to her husband. "Use Sage. They get along, and Grier won't suspect anything." And she knew Sage's loyalty belonged to her, friendship with her husband or not.

He nodded at her untouched plate. "Eat your toast. It'll settle your stomach."

After a quiet minute, he glanced up at her. "Can I ask you a question?"

"Yeah." She told him everything anyway... well, almost.

"Why Grier? What is it about this guy that you... that out of all the guys you could've had..." His skin flushed and he looked down at his plate."Why him?"

And of all the questions he could've asked, ones she had absolute, no doubt answers for, he'd picked the one she couldn't explain.

"I don't... I don't know." Grier had always been the guy she wanted, from the first minute she'd seen him when she was thirteen. No other boy when she was young or man when she got older measured up to him. He didn't have the most money and most of the time back then he'd acted like she was more of a burden than someone he could see himself with.

Her mind drifted back to that day in the changing room when she'd forced him to take her lingerie shopping. She'd been home from college, actually dating someone else, but she'd kissed Grier and known right then no other man would ever be the one for her.

"Dad thought it was a good idea." Her excuse was feeble. "He always liked him."

Hamilton nodded, but couldn't hide his doubt. The pursed lips. The narrow eyes. But it all vanished when he smiled. "Okay. But if he hurts you or the club, I'm going to kill him." He spoke with deadly truth, and she wouldn't have doubted him anyway. Hamilton kept his word, no matter what it cost him. And his loyalty was the stuff of legends. Thank God he was loyal to her.

FIONA'S HEAD DROPPED AGAIN, and she caught herself just before her forehead crashed into the keyboard. Damn. She hadn't been at work for more than a few hours and she could barely hold her eyes open. It had been three weeks of this shit and maybe she could've understood if she hadn't been sleeping so well at night. With Grier. Sleeping and nothing else. No matter how she tried to entice him. Oh, sure. He'd lick her or finger her or both until her body quivered and her stomach dropped out, then he rolled away to his own side of the bed and slept like the dead, no matter how many times she ground her pussy against him or took his dick into her hands.

Maybe he didn't like the slight bulge at her waist,

because she certainly didn't buy that whole poking the kid in the head bit, especially since she'd had the doctor explain in detail how they could safely screw their brains out. And still, he kept the damned thing locked up like Fort freaking Knox.

Almost worse yet, Hamilton still hadn't discovered anything they could use to prove Grier was telling the truth, no evidence he wasn't either. She leaned back and closed her eyes. A moment's peace without the nausea and fatigue would revive her, give her the strength to finish her work, to tally the money and make the required payouts. Just a minute.

"Hey, beautiful."

His mouth pressed against hers, and if this was a dream, she'd happily stay asleep and let it play out. And if her arms didn't weigh a thousand pounds each, she would have wrapped them around him and hung on, but instead, she let him spin her chair and kiss her again. "Hello." She murmured the word against his lips.

Her body seemed to be floating for a minute before he settled her on his lap in the chair behind her desk. He cradled her against him and brushed her hair off her forehead. "Do you want to go home? Take the rest of the day off?"

It sounded a little too much like heaven when she had so much work to do. But she snuggled closer. "I can't. I have to finish…" She waved her arm toward the desk, not worrying about the file folder in her top drawer, the one with Grier's background check, the details of a life he hadn't told her about. Or the file with the pictures of him with Dave, the one with him and Kye or the one of him coming onto the beach carrying a surfboard in Belize.

She knew they existed, even had a glimmer of recognition he would find them if he looked, but she didn't care. Right then, she wanted to go home, fall asleep in his arms, and let the day pass by unnoticed by either of them. And if club business wasn't so pressing, she would have insisted. Instead, she tilted her head down until her chin touched her chest.

God. She hated being weak, hated that her body would betray her with such forceful regularity. "I need help." The words slipped out, but she recognized the truth in them. "I can't do this anymore."

He tightened his arms around her. "Okay."

The softness of his voice broke her and her eyes welled with tears. Goddamned tears. "I can't take care of everything when I can't even stay awake, when my ankles are so swollen I can barely walk, and when my head hurts so bad the numbers are swimming in my brain." She sniffed and the dam on her thoughts burst open. "And I don't know if I can even trust you not to turn us all into your friends at the FBI, but I don't have anyone else I can ask without giving up control of the club." She hiccupped out a sob and wished she could take it all back and disappear.

But then he kissed the top of her head and squeezed her closer and she didn't give two imperial shits about anything but Grier. Jesus, the hormones were having their way with her today.

"Come on, Fifi. Let's go home."

"But…" Again, the desk full of orders and paperwork that needed attention.

"Fiona, I'll handle it." She loved the amount of authority he could summon. Usually, he only did it in the bedroom, and not at all recently, but the tone, the confidence, the command all warmed her inside. He stood and turned to put her in the chair, then crouched in front of her and removed her heels. Shoes she would happily toss off the top of the tallest building in town. He cradled her calf for an extra moment before he let her leg down. "Better?"

"Yeah." Somehow, he managed to make everything better. She smiled and ran her finger along his jaw. Maybe today she could convince him. She yawned again. After a nap.

A nice, long nap with her husband.

GRIER THREW the damned pen across the desk and stared at the numbers in front of him. He didn't have the foggiest of fucking ideas what any of this shit meant. He was an action man, could fire the wings off a fly at eighty paces, and nobody in the club could outride him, but put a page of math in front of him and it might as well be a foreign language. Still, he'd promised Fiona he would handle everything, and by God, he would. If it took all night, a night he would've preferred spending with her, but he'd left her with Hamilton who'd shown up just in time for her to remind Grier of his promise to see to club business.

He drained his fourth cup of coffee and tried to make sense of the page in front of him. Fuck. This wasn't working. Maybe after a break it would make more sense. He walked out of her office into the clubhouse. Sage stood against the bar talking to some Hell Kat Grier hadn't seen before and Autumn, who Grier knew all too well.

Jez handed him a beer as Autumn slithered off her stool and over to wrap her arms around his neck. Her shirt was cut low and her shorts high, and she ran her hand up his chest to his neck and into his hair. She jerked hard and mashed their mouths together.

Once upon a time, Autumn had rocked his world, at a time before he knew what he was doing, when he was too young to understand the complexities of sex and just sought out the pleasure of it. Now, he only wanted her away from him. He disentangled her arms and backed a step away. "I'm married."

She nodded and moved close enough to whisper in his ear. "I know, but word is the little wifey's sick. And I know you. You need a healthy woman who will do exactly what you tell her."

Again, he moved away. "Stop."

She backed off and raised both hands. "Fine."

Grier waited for her to wander away before he took the stool she'd vacated beside Sage. "You look like shit."

Yeah, well, he had a pregnant wife who hadn't quite grasped the concept of taking no for an answer, a club who may or may not have wanted him dead and questioned his loyalty at every turn, and enough paperwork he couldn't finish to build a mountain. "Thanks."

Sage nuzzled the Hell Kat with his chin, whispered something in her ear, and winked when she walked away. "What's up with you?"

Grier considered him. Sage was a guy with book smarts. A guy who could probably make sense of a line of numbers and come up with the answers Fiona needed. "I need your help."

Grier might not have been able to sort out the details himself, but he damned sure knew how to delegate.

* * *

GRIER CAME in the back door because the front creaked and groaned and while he hadn't quite gotten around to fixing it, he also didn't want to wake Fiona if she was sleeping. The TV was on and Fiona's laugh tinkled through the house. Grier came around the corner to find his wife and Hamilton seated close on the sofa, watching some old episodes of a sitcom, her head on his shoulder, his hand on a bowl of popcorn in her lap. Cozy.

And maybe because he was exhausted or maybe because she'd been on him like white on rice for weeks, and he'd consistently said no, or maybe because he was just jealous, he stood there contemplating all the different ways he wanted to kill Hamilton.

Instead of speaking, he stalked to the stairs and went up to shower. As he toweled off, she pushed the door open and walked in. "Do we have a problem?"

The stream of water had done nothing to soothe his anger or quell his rage. She'd been down there all over Hamilton, probably after they'd… and now, she stood in front of him, all innocence and wide eyes. "Nope."

"He's been my friend all my life." She took a step closer. "And you're the one who left him here with me."

As cliché as it sounded, Grier couldn't believe his ears. She was blaming him? "I left him here to make sure you were okay. Not for… anything else."

She smiled, took the towel and tossed it behind her. "You're cute when you're jealous."

"I'm not jealous." Maybe a little, but damned if he planned to admit it to her.

"Okay, you're cute when I'm horny." She stripped off her clothes and his resolve weakened. Disappeared. And no damned way could he hide it with her standing in front of him and his towel on the floor behind her.

"Fiona…"

But she'd wrapped her leg around his hip and latched her mouth onto his. She ground her hips as she sucked his tongue into her mouth. He felt the pull deep in his groin and his dick twitched, seeking the heat of her pussy.

She pulled back enough to stare at him for a second. "Please, Grier. Please."

Her soft tone, the way her body melded to his, the fingers gripping his shoulders, and the warmth of her naked body against his made the decision as if he'd ever had the choice. He moved to let the wall support her as he drove into her. "Oh, God." It had been too long. He wouldn't be able to last, wouldn't be able to hold back, especially with her lips sucking his neck and her hips bucking, her whimpers, her… everything.

"Come for me, Grier. Now."

The walls of her pussy clenched around his cock, and

he let go, spiraled away until only Fiona existed. "Holy shit."

She slid down the front of him, arms around his waist as she smiled. "Well, if our kid has a dented head, we'll know why."

She had such magic in her she'd managed to make him forget the reason he hadn't been making love to her every minute of every day since they'd been together. Until now. "Fiona."

"Just kidding. The doctor said…"

"I know." Not that he understood the science of it any better than he'd been able to grasp the math earlier. And he resolved that if he did nothing else in his life, he would make sure his kid finished school with grades that weren't just ones to pass him onto the next year. His kid would study and be smart, make something of himself.

"Come on. Let's go to bed so I can make fun of you for being jealous of Ham."

"I wasn't jealous." He knew she wouldn't cheat on him. With Hamilton. Or with anyone else. So it damned well couldn't have been jealousy.

"Okay." She shrugged, but her smirk said she didn't believe him any more than he believed himself. "Let's go to bed anyway."

5

Fiona knew Grier wouldn't do anything to sell out the club, knew he would die protecting her and the baby. What she didn't know was why he was in one of the warehouses with Dave's "wife" and two other men who could only have been FBI.

Sage handed her the binoculars, and she adjusted the lenses, aimed at a window. Damned if she could see anything though. "What's he doing in there?"

"I don't know. I couldn't see a damned thing."

"You're sure no one saw you? No one knows you followed him here?"

Her car, hidden in the trees, couldn't have been seen, but no telling where Sage had parked his bike. "No. My bike's down the road. I came here on foot just as they all went inside."

This was a Demon warehouse, where they'd stored

merchandise and trucks since she was a little girl. Why the hell would he pick here for a meet and greet with the FBI? She clenched her teeth. Things had been going so well these last few weeks… months actually since she'd finally convinced Grier to take over more of the operations at the club and since he'd finally started seeing her as his wife instead of as an incubator with tits.

"Fuck."

"Should we go in? Bust up the party?"

No. *They* shouldn't. "Go back to the clubhouse and wait for me." When he didn't move, she shot him a glare. "Go. I'm just gonna wait here for them to come out."

"Fiona…"

"Sage, I know, okay? Husband or not, if he's fucking the club, I'll bring him back to you, but he won't talk to me if you're standing there with your chest puffed out ready to pounce. The only way this goes right is if I'm here alone." She put her best tough-girl spin on the words, but her heart ached at the thought of having to turn Grier over to the club, but more than likely, she would have to.

"I know that. I'm not questioning you. I just know if it was me, I wouldn't want to go through something like this alone." He dropped a hand on her shoulder.

Damn. Not folding herself in half and crying on his shoulder took every ounce of strength she had, but she kept her head up and her shoulders back. "I'll be fine." She swallowed hard against the lie.

"Okay. I'll see you at the clubhouse, but if you aren't there in an hour, I'm calling you. And if you don't answer, I'm bringing all the guys back with me. And we won't be hiding in some damned trees with binoculars." He raised his eyebrows and waited for her nod before he climbed out of the car and disappeared behind the car.

Fiona waited a couple of seconds before she opened the door, a couple more before she clung to the shadows beside the building near the door Sage had pointed out where Grier walked in with the feds. She had two choices, burst in and make her presence known or try to sneak through and catch whatever she could of the conversation.

She tried the door handle and it screeched with just a half-turn. Burst in it was. She yanked the door open and hurried inside. Four heads turned to look at her and Grier shoved whatever he'd been holding into his back pocket. "Well, what do we have here?"

Grier hung his head. "Babe, it's all right. This isn't what you think."

She ignored him and walked over to stand in front of the woman who'd "leaned" on her when her "husband" burned up in a Screaming Demon truck. She didn't have words to quantify the amount of deception, to justify the lie. "I comforted you."

The woman lifted her chin and stared at Fiona, no remorse, not a glimmer of apology. Fiona made a fist and swung it around. The smack of knuckles against cheekbones as satisfying as it was painful. Grier rushed forward and grabbed her by the shoulders, pulling her away and shielding her behind him as the other woman rebounded and advanced.

"She's pregnant." His voice was calm, deadly, a warning, and a redundancy since her belly arrived in a room three to four seconds before the rest of her.

"What the hell is she doing here?" One of the men in black suits shook his head at Grier. "Our deal's with you."

"I'm in it now," Fiona stepped around Grier. No way did she need him to protect her from some suits with badges. "And somebody needs to start explaining before this place starts filling up with Screaming Demons." One day she'd forgotten her watch when it would have looked so dramatic to have checked it right then. Dammit.

None of the agents spoke, and she turned her head toward Grier. He didn't look away, but half-smiled. "Well, funny enough, the FBI needs me." And likely whatever he'd put into his pocket was a part of it.

Their voices echoed off the high ceilings in the warehouse, empty except for a couple of trucks. The concrete floor made her legs ache, but she remained ramrod straight as she waited. After this was resolved, she would find out why the hell a warehouse that should have been full to the ceiling sat empty, but first she had to deal with FBI agents and double-dealing husbands.

"Needs you how?"

He pulled a picture from his back pocket and handed it to Fiona. She stared at the black-and-white image wishing for a little more light. "You recognize anybody in that picture?"

Of course she did. Her father. One-eye Jim. Hamilton. And a couple of guys she didn't know. They seemed to be friendly, laughing and smoking outside the clubhouse. But what she noticed more than anything else, was the scar under the open cut of one of the guys she didn't know. A brand. Just like the one Sedotal had had.

Her stomach twisted and the world tilted. Her legs went weak. She didn't have any damned idea what this picture meant. She only knew she couldn't catch her breath.

Grier watched her and she worked to keep it together. One deep, as deep as she could get anyway, breath followed by another. "I don't… what is this?"

"Your dad and this guy," Grier pointed to the guy with the scar, "Do you know him?"

Fiona stared at the picture. "I don't think so." But a part of her brain wouldn't let go of… something. A familiarity. "Maybe. Who is he?"

Dave's "wife" took a step forward then, at Fiona's glare, moved back to her original spot. "His name is Willy Carr." She sighed as if having to explain was beneath her. "Former founding member of the Screaming Demons. His son's name is Tyler Sedotal."

It was a lot to digest. Too much. Fiona looked from one agent to the other, took in the suits and ties, the guns holstered just under their arms, the woman in the pantsuit with the tight white shirt with buttons open enough to show her ample chest.

"Where did you get this?" She waved the picture like a flag then jerked it away when one of the men in black tried to take it from her. Her look, one she'd practiced for years, a warning and he stepped to his original spot.

"Special Agent Kern… um, Dave, took it from your dad's house. When Mr. Owen called and asked for this meeting," Fiona's head jerked toward Grier as the FBI woman continued talking, "he specifically asked about Tyler Sedotal." She nodded to the photo. "We've been looking for all these men for a while."

"Why?"

"Obviously we knew where to find your father, Jim Caprici, and Damian Hamilton, but Willy Carr has been in the wind for a while. Then his son surfaced at the Demon clubhouse." She clasped her hands together in front of her. "Carr is dangerous. Runs guns, drugs, women. But he's gone off-grid." She shot Grier a look. "Obviously, we want to find him."

Fiona scoffed and rolled her eyes. "Obviously." So they expected Grier to help? Or the club? No fucking way. The Screaming Demons would never get into bed with the FBI. No matter what.

The woman cleared her throat and ran a hand along the top of her head where her hair had been pulled back into a severe bun. Fiona didn't want Sedotal found. She wanted him dead. But she also had her own group of men to accomplish this task. She didn't need government assistance.

Grier inched closer. "Fiona, I can handle this. You shouldn't…"

He went to the FBI. Not only was it dangerous, but if the guys found out… "Are you trying to get yourself killed?" She hissed the words from between clenched teeth.

"No. I want to find Sedotal." His voice, reasonable and soft, further inflamed her sense of club loyalty.

It didn't matter if he'd called the FBI to report a murder of someone in the club by a Yeti. Again, Grier had betrayed the club with his little tryst with the FBI, and the reason didn't matter. The FBI in its entirety was neither friend nor ally. And he knew, probably as well as anyone else, calling them would get him killed.

Fiona had heard enough. She didn't need information provided by a bunch of feds. And she didn't need a husband who would go behind her back and ask those sons of bitches for help, either. She tamped down the ache in her heart with a burst of anger. If she could hang onto her fury, it would get her through the heartache.

"I'm going home." She glared at her husband. "You should probably stay out and look for Sedotal. Wouldn't want him getting away. And if you play your cards right, maybe your new friends will get you one of those shiny badges all of your own." Fiona wanted to crumple the picture into a ball and throw it in his face, but instead, she folded it in half and shoved it into her open collar. She wanted to look at it, investigate it for herself. And show it to Hamilton.

* * *

Grier watched Fiona walk out. The slam of the heavy metal door didn't just say she was angry, it screamed it with a screech of steel on concrete. "Fuck."

"Is she going to be a problem?" Agent Demuer, former military with the build and haircut to prove it, put both hands on his hips and stared at Grier.

Of course she was going to be a problem. An angry, semi-violent when she had to be leader of a badass motorcycle club wasn't going to sit back and tolerate one of her men, husband or not, going to the FBI for help. Hell to pay was a generous description of what he could expect when he returned home. If he even had a home. Currently, he couldn't say.

"No. She'll think it over and…" He shrugged. Probably she'd think it over and call in the firing squad herself. An image of himself standing against a wall with Hamilton and One-eye holding machine guns locked and loaded flashed through his mind.

"Tyler Sedotal is missing right now." Demuer stared Grier down, but if he thought he was one bit intimidating he was wrong. "And we know you've been looking for him. If you find him, can we expect a phone call?"

No. They could probably expect a gun battle. "You bet."

"There was a compound, a camp, years ago. We have it under surveillance, but it's been quiet. No men in. No men out." Agent Billings, Dave's "wife", stared at Grier. "It was Carr's hideaway. Where he kept the women and the drugs."

"So what's the point in watching it if no one's using it?"

"Funny you should ask. A delivery arrived there yesterday. Toilet paper, coffee grounds, dried fruit."

Grier chuckled. "And you think Sedotal is stupid enough to use the internet to order his supplies and have them delivered to a place he probably knows you're sitting on?" Sedotal wasn't dumb enough to leave a paper trail. "Why not just walk into a Walmart? He could be in and out and back in the wind before you ever knew he'd been there. Leaving a paper trail seems kind of dumb."

She cocked her head and considered him. "Not if he's trying to be found."

"Easier ways to do that, too."

"Look, it's a lead. It's what we have." Demuer crossed his arms. "Now you."

"Now me? What?" They couldn't possibly think Grier would be exchanging information.

"We lost Kern." He produced a file from, it seemed, thin air and opened it to pull out a picture of Grier with Dave, the same picture Fiona had shown him but from a different angle. "And you were the last one to see him alive."

Fuck. They had him. He couldn't afford to get locked up, to leave Fiona pregnant and unprotected. "What do you want?"

"Damian Hamilton."

Grier worked to keep his face blank. "No." Aside from being a member of the club, Hamilton was Fiona's best friend.

"Hamilton killed Agent Kern."

"Isn't that who you plan to accuse me of killing?"

Wasn't that what using the picture was about? "How do you know?"

The agent pulled out another picture. Hamilton on a bike, casual, gun drawn, Dave's hands up. "What we didn't release, the information we have, is that Agent Kern died from a gunshot wound to the head. He was put into the truck, and Hamilton set it on fire." He pulled out another picture that told the whole story - Hamilton lighting the truck on fire. Not only did they have Hamilton on murder, they had the club on running stolen merchandise stuffed with illegal drugs. And he would've bet anything he owned and a bunch of shit he didn't, that fact would come up eventually.

Fuck. Fuck. Fuck. Why would Hamilton do it? Unless he knew Dave was FBI. Which meant he'd been following Grier? Fucking Hamilton. So, Goddamned gung-ho for the club. He would've known the truck would have been a sacrifice, but one they could make for the sake of weeding out a rat.

Grier stared at the photo. It wasn't Hamilton's bike. Or Hamilton's neck tattoo. He knew because Hamilton didn't have a neck tattoo. The image was blurry, and at first look, he'd been fooled. But this wasn't Hamilton. He folded the picture and put it in his pocket. They would never have come here and even showed him the picture if they didn't have a copy, hanging on a board somewhere in a police station. "Hamilton won't come easy. Not with me."

Demuer smiled, but pure evil emanated off this guy. "You'll figure it out. Or you can serve his time." He glanced at the other agents. "What's the term for killing law enforcement these days? Life, right? Without parole?" He cocked an eyebrow at Grier. "I'm sure your kid'll understand the club was more important."

Grier turned and walked out. No point in listening to this asshole when he had his facts all wrong. Besides, his honey-do list kept growing by the minute. Not only did he have to find Sedotal, he had to figure out who was setting up Hamilton, who was targeting the club, how to take that look out of Fiona's eyes, and if he had any time left, he had to figure out how to be a father. Should've stayed in Belize.

6

All she'd wanted was a little help. Some protection from the mad men trying to drag the club back to the depths from which her father had managed to pull it. Now she had a husband, one she'd picked for fuck's sake, in cahoots with the FBI.

"Hamilton?" He sat at the bar next to her, sipping a beer and watching the new Wall Kat lap dance a very drunk Sage.

He turned his stool to face her. "What's up?"

She looked around. Jez behind the bar. Dale and Jim at a table. Sage and the Wall Kat. Autumn hovering near them, pretending to wipe down tables though she'd been cleaning the same table since Fiona walked in. A guy she didn't recognize, big, Hamilton big, fondling another Wall Kat while he stared at Fiona.

"Who's that?" She nodded to the hulking dude with

his hand up the Wall Kat's shirt.

"Name's Kale something or other. Came from down south. One of your dad's old buddies."

The neck tattoo stretched around a throat as big as Fiona's thigh, and he had Hamilton's hair. If she hadn't clearly seen his face, she might've mistaken him for Hamilton. "What's he doing here?"

"Heard Max died. Came in a couple of months ago to pay his respects. Never left." Hamilton shrugged and emptied his glass then nodded to Jez for another.

Months? And she'd never noticed him? "For a guy who's here to pay his respects, I would think I would've met him."

Hamilton cocked an eyebrow. "Yeah. That's a little odd." He ran his finger around the rim of his glass. "You want me to get rid of him?"

When Hamilton asked if she wanted someone *gotten rid of,* there wasn't an easy way to tell whether he meant ask the guy to leave or something a little more permanent. "No. I want you to watch him. Be friends, Hamilton." She ended on a smile. "For now."

Hamilton chuckled. "How many eyes do you think I have, Fiona? I'm already watching your boy."

And yet he hadn't mentioned a damned thing about a meet with the FBI. Thank God he'd been switching nights with Sage on Grier-watch. "Yeah. Leave Sage on Grier, and you stay with that guy." And what the hell kind of name was Kale? "I want to know why he hasn't gone back south yet." And again, Grier was out there, somewhere, unwatched, unmonitored, making God only knew what kind of deals with the FBI. Fuck. She sighed.

* * *

JEZ SET a pizza in front of Hamilton. He shoved the pan in front of Fiona. "Eat."

"All right." These days, no one had to tell her twice to shovel in the food.

"Where's lover boy? Sage said he left him with you."

And as quickly as her appetite developed, it disappeared. She dropped her piece of pizza back onto the metal pan. "He's fine. He's, um… out." Telling Hamilton that Grier was "out" with the FBI would only assure her husband's swift, immediate, and largely painful disappearance and death. She'd have a patch of earth to show her baby as his father. And while she knew it had to happen, she needed a few days to get in line with the thought.

"Out alone?"

"It's fine." The quiver in her voice betrayed the surety of her words. "Really. He's, um, looking for Sedotal." In his own back-handed way, she supposed. A totally out-of-bounds, would-get-himself-killed-for-it way.

"Mm." Hamilton took a swig of his beer then looked at her long and hard, his eyes pointed into hers. "Fi, I've got you no matter what, okay? You don't have to go through any of this alone."

She nodded, too choked on emotion to speak. He'd been her first protector. Her first friend. The first man, beside her father, she'd ever trusted. And for the thousandth time, she had to wonder why she'd chosen Grier over Hamilton. Before her reasons had seemed so clear. Now, not so much.

"Now eat. Heirs to the throne can't be born scrawny and thin." He pushed the pan further in front of her.

She nibbled at the piece she'd previously discarded as her mind whirred with all she knew. But one thought pushed all others to the rear. Grier had somehow managed to align himself with the FBI. What she didn't know was when. She knew the details of his association with Dave. That Max had set it up. Presumably so if the club discovered it, Max would have deniability. And it made sense. But going to the FBI now? That didn't jive. And she'd be the one who would have to call for his death.

"You okay?"

She would have answered, reassured him, but the door to the clubhouse slammed open and Grier stood just inside, his eyes dark with fury, his face a grimace. She turned and waited. The music stopped. Sage stood.

Hamilton stood. And the fondler pushed away his Wall Kat. He didn't quite make it to his feet, but that was a lot of man to pull from a chair if there wasn't a need. Still, his eyes didn't so much as twitch or blink, and for a moment Fiona stared. She could almost smell the danger reeking off this guy.

"Grier." Hamilton had the presence of mind to hold out his hand to stop Grier from advancing on Fiona while she continued staring at Kale.

Hamilton had one hand at his back on the butt of the gun he kept in his waistband. She put her hand on his arm. "I think this might be a personal matter." Even as she spoke the words, the bitterness of the lie burned on her tongue. She moved around Hamilton. "Come on, *honey*, let's talk it out."

She took a tentative step toward Grier who still glared, not so much at her, but at everyone around her. Sage appeared at her side then moved to throw an arm around Grier. "Come on, big fella. Let's have us a drink and a talk?"

For as drunk as he sounded, Sage's eyes were missing the glaze that came with alcohol overload. Grier's, by comparison, flamed with anger. He shoved Sage away and stared at the Hamilton look-alike. "You!"

Everything else happened in seconds, a blur of motion and fists, sidesteps, by Grier, thank God, and shouts. Hamilton shielded her long enough for Jez to pull her behind the bar, then joined the fray. A TV fell. Tables were upended. Glasses shattered. Bottles thrown. But the sound, every punch rang through her head. Each grunt and shout echoed off the high ceiling. Until it ended with Hamilton holding Kale, both arms behind his back and Sage on top of Grier whose face was pressed into the floor under the force of Sage's knee.

Now it was time to sort this fucking mess. She came out from her hiding spot and walked around the bar. "Let him up." Sage stood then lifted Grier by his arm. A tornado could have blown through the place and left less devastation, but she didn't care about that. Instead, she jabbed her finger into Grier's chest. "What the hell is wrong with you?"

He reached behind his back and Sage grabbed him again. Grier struggled free. "I'm not fucking armed." But he was bleeding from a gash over his eye and a split in his lip. "There's a picture in my pocket."

Sage pulled it out and handed it to Fiona. She nodded at Sage who released Grier again, but didn't move away. Fiona glanced at the photo. Hamilton lighting the truck on fire. She stared from him to the picture. That he'd gotten it from the FBI didn't mean as much as what it showed. "Hamilton?"

Grier tried to move closer, but Sage held him back. "Not Ham. It's that fucker!" He jabbed a finger toward the man who lunged with force almost enough to break Hamilton's hold. But not quite. And thank God.

Grier, on the other hand, was not so restrained, and he made it to Kale before Sage could pull him back. He put his shoulder down and barreled into Kale who toppled backward onto Hamilton's. Kale rolled off and pinned Grier then jabbed with a meaty fist into Grier's jaw with one hand and his temple with the other. Grier's head jerked from one side to the other. Hamilton pulled Kale off again. And Grier, whose face would be unrecognizable by morning, made it to his feet.

He spat blood onto the floor. "I don't know why. But it's him."

Fiona stared at the picture harder, looked for anything that would differentiate the blur in the picture from Hamilton. Same height. Same coloring. But the blob of black on the neck, that wasn't Hamilton. Grier was right. Hopefully, no one questioned why he had the picture or where he'd gotten it. Hopefully, the bloodlust would be too strong to allow for conscious thought.

She strode up to Kale, safe thanks to Hamilton's hold on him. "Who are you really?"

He glared at her, spat. "Fuck you."

She walked as if she didn't have a care to the back of the bar and pulled a pistol from where Jez kept it in case of emergency. The sound of the slide pushing a shell into the chamber proved the point she wanted to make, but not so much as when she pressed the barrel against Kale's forehead. "No. Fuck you."

He laughed. "You think you're so safe here. So protected. All these puny bitches at your beck and call. You don't know shit."

Fiona shrugged. "So why don't you tell me. We'll call it a deathbed confession." She pushed his forehead back with the gun.

"Your boyfriend is playing footsies with the FBI and your driver was an undercover special agent. I did you a favor." Nothing earthshattering to her, but not everyone in the room had the benefit of the same information system she did. "The Screaming Demons are a joke. Trying to go legit. Trying to take yourselves out of guns and drugs and whores."

"We never..." Oh, God. They'd never run women. Her father wouldn't have... Not the problem at hand. She cleared her mind and stared. If Kale kept talking, Grier wouldn't last through the night. She looked up at Hamilton. "Get him down to the cells." The cells underneath the club hadn't been used in... as far as she knew, ever, but right now she needed them.

Hamilton and Jim wrestled Kale out the door and every other eye in the room honed in on Fiona, standing beside Grier. She put the gun down at her side and glanced at her husband. Her head and back ached, her heart hurt and she had a million things to decide in the next few minutes. But to do it, she had to keep Grier alive. For a little while at least. She nodded to Sage. "Him, too."

It was for his protection as much as to punish him.

"Fiona!"

Grier struggled against Sage's hold until One-eye Jim crossed the floor to use the butt of his gun against the back of Grier's head to knock him out. Was it wrong to be grateful?

* * *

JEZ USED sandpaper to clean the cut over his eye. Probably just rubbing alcohol on a piece of gauze but felt like sandpaper. He winced and jerked away as she attacked again with her "help".

"Easy, goddamn, Jez."

She glared and jabbed the gauze back at his face. "I've known that girl since she was three years old." Not news. "She was raised to take this club over and lead it into the future so we all had something, big money to share in." Again, nothing he didn't already know. "And you, little son of a bitch, are not going to take her down."

He would have answered, might have even looked at her, but currently his jaw hurt too bad to open, and his eyes were swelling with an alarming speed. He sat quietly absorbing the pain she seemed intent to inflict.

"And where's your head at?" As if to answer her own question, she slapped the side of his skull. "You have a baby on the way and you're talking to the FBI? You want your kid born in jail? Shipped off to some foster family? You, as well as anyone, should know the dangers there. You want that for your kid?"

Grier didn't owe anyone an explanation. He'd done what needed doing, found the rat inside their club. Probably would've helped to know who was getting Demon information from Kale Riznewski, but that would come. In time. If they let him live past tonight. He had hope. Why would Jez be cleaning his wounds if they just planned to take him out and kill him?

"I won't let anything happen to her." It was the most he could manage and as he spoke, his head swam, a haze of black closing in. He probably, at the very least, had a concussion, some broken knuckles. That fucking Kale's jaw must have been forged in steel or carved in some granite. "I love her."

"You have a funny damned way of showing it." His eyes closed and he swayed, but she held him up. "Don't you go to sleep on me, boy. They'll be coming for you soon."

"Who?" The word sounded far away, but a reasonable enough question.

"You know who. Hamilton and Fiona, Sage and Jim. The boys who want an explanation."

He mumbled incoherent words. "Sedotal. Rape. Hamilton on the hook." Incoherent if the story wasn't running on a reel-to-reel in his mind. His brain filled in the missing details but he couldn't seem to get it all out to make her understand.

"What?"

Grier tried again. "I can't find Sedotal. So, I called the FBI, asked for help. He tried to rape her, Jez." She put her hands down, stopped her "mothering" and stared. "He isn't the kind of guy who will stop coming for her." A light clicked in his head. "When did Kale show up here? Before or after Sedotal disappeared?"

"After?"

"Doesn't matter. He killed Dave. But the FBI thinks it's Ham. And if I don't hand him over, I'm going down for it." The details were all there. He just needed to sort them so they made sense.

"Did you kill Dave?"

"No. Kale did. But they think it's Ham."

Jez cocked her head. "I could see that. In a dark room, it would be easy to mistake one for the other."

"And the picture was taken with a night vision lens maybe. It's blurry and dark." Every word he said cost him pain and breath, but he needed someone on his side, someone who believed in him. And since it couldn't be his wife, maybe he could use the woman closest to her. "But it isn't Ham. The tattoo.

We need to find out who Kale is working for, why he's here."

The cell was mostly dark except a caged lightbulb overhead. And empty except for one wooden bench bolted to the floor. Not even a toilet. If he couldn't talk his way out of there, it was going to be a very long night.

"Jez, she's in danger. The whole club is. Not from the FBI but from Sedotal and Kale's people. Whoever they are. They set the fire and framed Hamilton, shot Dave and planted Kale here to make sure I'm nowhere near Fiona so they can get to her."

Jez chuckled. "For a guy who just got his ass handed to him, you sure are cocky about your ability to protect Fiona."

"I would die for her." For all he knew, he was already dead.

She closed the first aid kit. "Let's just hope it doesn't come to that."

"Will you help me?"

She stopped at the door and stared at him. Jez didn't have to worry about him chasing her out even if he could somehow manage to stand. He'd woken to find his hands zip-tied behind his back and his ankle caught in a steel cuff attached to a chain bolted to the floor. "What happens to you is up to Fiona. You caught the bastard down the hall. Maybe that'll count for something."

After she left, he had nothing to do but hope so.

7

Something about seeing Grier chained in one of the basement cells made Fiona undeniably sad. The cell, once upon a time a maintenance operations room when this was an up and running factory, was concrete wall on three sides and the door had been replaced with actual steel bars, welded and reinforced in the shop way back when the Demons first found this place. When everything went to a vote. Before her father had turned this into his own form of monarchy or dictatorship. Before she was born anyway.

From the camera inside the cell which transmitted to her computer, she watched Grier reclined casually against the wall, as if she didn't have his next breath in her hands, the power to extinguish him within her reach. Every hope she'd ever had for them had vanished as soon as she walked in the supply warehouse the night before. But damned if she wanted him dead. Especially after the story he'd told Jez. *I would die for her.*

The plan hadn't been to send Jez down. She'd wanted to go herself, to talk to him, to touch him one last time, but Hamilton and Sage spent a lot of time and energy helping her rethink it. Hamilton leaned against the wall in one corner of her office, and Sage sat in the chair in front of her.

No one had spoken in hours. She glanced away from the monitor at Sage. "You know him. What do you think?"

Sage shook his head. "I don't know. He's killing himself trying to find Sedotal."

"He called the FBI. Went to them and everyone in this room and everyone out there-" Hamilton jerked his thumb toward the door, "-knows the feds don't give shit away for free. What did he have to give them? What do they want in return?"

Thanks to the conversation with Jez, she knew exactly what the FBI wanted. They wanted Hamilton. As angry as she was, as sad as she was, she wanted Grier, to feel his arms around her, to rest her head against his chest, to tell him she'd felt the baby move.

To tell, or not to tell. That was the question. If she knew too much, the club would think she was in this as deep as Grier. Hell, they probably already did. If she knew too little, they would think her incompetent. And if she went too easy on Grier while everything was so uncertain, they would think her weak or led by her pussy. She tried to channel a little Max, the man they'd all followed without question, the man who put business first.

Fiona slapped her hands on the desk and a pile of papers fluttered in the slight breeze the motion created. "All right. Send Jim and Dale out for rent. Get Nate and Griff to bring me Grier, and you two get Kale on the hook." Not an actual hook. More of a screw in the foot kind of thing but her dad had always called it *on the hook*. Her father, inspired by something he'd seen on TV, created it to help lift the truth out of those less than willing to communicate.

"What do you want us to do once we have him ready?"

She smiled. "Wait for me. This is a job I'm going to want to handle myself."

"And if Kale resists?" Hamilton's smile said he hoped Kale put up a fight.

She shrugged. "Handle it. But I want him alive." There was something raw and primal in her words, a strength and determination she could have only gotten from Max.

As Sage left, Hamilton hung back for a second. "I should be in here with you."

The worry in his eyes warmed her. "I'll be okay." She

opened the drawer and pulled out a pearl-handled Glock. "Daddy made sure I'm a good shot. And if Grier breathes wrong, I'm not afraid to prove it."

Her words were braver than she felt, and her stomach clenched at the thought of having to shoot Grier when all she really wanted was to throw herself against him and press kisses everywhere she could reach.

She closed her eyes and waited, firming up her resolve not to want him, not to need him, or love him or care even one iota whether or not he walked out of her office or had to be zipped in a bag and carried out.

But her resolve faded when Nate pushed him through the door. Oh, God. His face, bruised, swollen, misshapen, made her heart ache. Grier limped toward the chair, his hands still bound behind him. Nate waited inside the door. "Give us a minute."

"Fiona…"

"Go." Her tone left no more room for argument. "I can handle a cripple who can't see out of one eye." All this concern made her weary. She didn't look at Grier again until Nate closed the door behind him. "This is a fucking mess." She ran her hands through her hair, thankful for the desk between them.

He nodded. "Sorry I didn't clean up first. I've been a little tied up."

His words lisped out but he attempted a smile that

faltered into a grimace. She looked away, unable to stand his pain. "They're going to kill you."

"I know." He shrugged. "Do I get a last meal? Maybe a last piss? It's been a long night." He glanced at her. "I'll let you hold it for me."

She chuckled with the absurdity of a man ten minutes from death behaving this way. "I don't think you want me anywhere near your dick right now. It might not survive so well."

"At least bury me with it, okay?"

"Grier..."

He swallowed and his open eye brimmed with tears. "I love you. I know it doesn't mean anything to you anymore, but I do. And I would rather die than hurt you."

Pretty words. That was all they were. And crying was a nice touch. She sighed. "Why didn't you just tell me? Why'd you go to them?"

He shook his head. Instead of looking at her, he glanced out the window. "You're my wife, and I didn't protect you." There was actual pain in his voice. And while she couldn't say for certain that it didn't stem from his physical ails, he'd been joking only a minute ago. "I sent you home, Fiona. And that son of a bitch is out there somewhere, waiting for his chance to come back and go at you again. I've looked. I've talked to everyone I can find and I got nothing." He sat up straighter. "I called them because I'm desperate, and I'm tired of letting you down."

"Grier." But he'd lowered his head and wouldn't look at her again. She opened her mouth to try again. "Grier. It wasn't your fault, okay? I should've known about him. Max would've known." He would've sniffed out the traitor, and he would've known Sedotal was hellbent on hurting Fiona. She'd been so busy trying to prove herself, she had let the details slip by. "I don't know what to do about you."

"Max would blow my kneecaps off then string me up and let the guys use me as a piñata." He nodded to the gun on the corner of her desk, handle toward her, ready to be picked up and aimed. "Are we going to be doing that?"

She, too, stared at the gun. Even if she wanted to, which she didn't, she couldn't shoot Grier. The father of her baby. The man she loved. "No." She opened the drawer and replaced the gun in its velvet-lined spot. "Did the FBI tell you anything?"

"Yeah."

She waited for him to tell her, but he shifted his shoulders and resumed a casual slouch. A really casual slouch for a guy with no future with his wife. Even if she kept him alive, he would have to leave the club. "Are you going to tell me?"

"Fiona..."

Oh, this protecting her business was getting a little old. "Grier, they will kill you, but not if I give them something else. Not if I tell them where to find Sedotal and explain what happened." It would mean giving them all the details, and she would, if it meant keeping Grier alive.

He nodded. "There's a camp. It's been empty for years but today a delivery driver brought supplies. But the FBI is sitting on it. They think Sedotal or Carr is going to show up there."

"And they're just going to let us run in there, get Sedotal and be on our way?"

Grier chuckled. "Probably not, but we've done a lot of shit under those noses over the years. Dragging one maniac out and stringing him up in the trees shouldn't be a problem."

If it worked, if she could give the guys a reason Grier was there and a retribution to spend, maybe… "So, where's this camp?"

"I don't know yet. But I think Kale does." She still had the picture he'd brought back from his meet with the FBI and the one she'd brought with her. "He killed Dave, torched the truck, and set up Hamilton. I don't really think he's Demon material." As she stared at him, wondering how much of what he said was true, he sighed. "Fiona, when did all this start going sideways? Think about it."

She had. "When Max died."

He nodded. "Kind of." At least he wasn't outright blaming her. "When Sedotal showed up, the trucks started going missing, guys started leaving, and when you busted him out of here, Kale came on the scene."

She couldn't verify his timeline with so many details in cyclone mode in her mind. One deep centering breath later, she was back on track. "You went to the FBI."

"Because I love you, Fiona. As ridiculous as it is, I love you."

That hurt. "Why ridiculous?"

He shook his head. "Well, first, you locked me in a cell overnight. We can start there and work our way back through the ridiculous milestones of our marriage, if you want." When she didn't answer, he swiped his tongue over the cut in his lower lip. "Maybe because you, my *wife*, are seriously considering handing me over to a bunch of angry bikers who will kill me one piece at a time. And I'm considering letting you because it'll mean they'll always stand beside you and protect you no matter what."

But ridiculous? Grier was on a roll. Although she couldn't really deny anything he'd said. She held up her hand. "Okay. I got the point. Ridiculous." Not a word she ever wanted to hear again either. "But you're wrong. I'm not going to kill you or hand you over to the guys. We just need to come up with something else that will satisfy them." And she loved him back, with all her heart. Why else would she consider lying to the club?

* * *

GRIER LIMPED into the shop behind Fiona. He couldn't see out of his right eye and his left was only half-open. His guts ached and he was pretty sure he'd never walk upright again, but he had to face the music and no way could he let Fiona deal with it alone.

And oh, his wife. Power looked good on her. She walked taller. Stood straighter. Held a gun like she'd been born with one in her hand. And it was hot.

She walked to the center of the room and pushed Sage away from a barefoot Kale. He was strapped standing against a board that held him suspended a foot off the ground. Jesus, this fucking guy was huge. And he struggled against the leather restraints. If he somehow managed to get out of this torture contraption, he would kill them all. Probably with his bare hands.

Grier looked at the restraints. Leather. Thick. Buckled so that Kale could barely move.

Fiona stood in front of him, arms crossed, gun gripped in her palm, barrel peeking out under her left elbow. "Who are you?"

"Fuck you, bitch."

As calm as if she was serving him an iced tea, she turned the gun and shot a hole through his hand. He winced, flinched a little, but stared at her with as much hate in his eyes as Grier had ever seen. "No. Fuck you. I can do this all day. How long do you think you can?"

Grier waited at the fringe of the Demons, fascinated, watching his wife handle club business in a way that would have made her father proud. Hamilton stood on one side of Kale and Sage on the other, although Sage had taken a step back when Fiona fired her gun.

The gun at her side caught the light and reflected it back as she put it down at her side. "Now, I want to know who you are and what you're doing in my clubhouse." She leaned in. "Little tip. I'm not going for a hand next time." She walked closer and pressed the gun into his dick. "Now, you have ten seconds to start talking." As Kale struggled against the restraints at his hands and feet, twisting and pulling, Fiona began the countdown. "Nine." Sage turned the screw over Kale's left foot. "Eight." Hamilton took a turn with the right screw. "Seven." Sage again. Kale breathed deeper but didn't cry out. The crowd around Grier grew restless, fidgeting, murmuring among themselves. They wanted blood, but more they wanted to know Fiona was causing this guy pain. And denying them heightened their need.

But Grier watched, fascinated by his wife. It was like

a choreographed dance with Fiona keeping time. As the blood dripped from Kale's feet, he hung his head.

"Six." This time Sage and Hamilton worked together. "Five."

"Stop!" Kale lifted his head and stared at Fiona. "He's going to come for you." His voice was labored and his breaths huffed out between each word.

"Who? Tyler?"

"And Willy."

"Willy Carr?"

Kale lifted his head to glare at Fiona. "No, Willy Wonka."

She jabbed the butt of the gun into his crotch and he yelped. Wasn't a big enough man in the world to withstand that pain without a reaction. "Why?"

"I don't know. Willy sent me here when you shot Ty. He said to watch you and him." He brought his eyes up to Grier. "They're going to get you both."

Fiona's head jerked back and she brought the gun away from his dick to hold in front of her mouth. Before he thought to step forward, she'd raised the gun and shot Kale.

She breathed in deep then let it out in a whoosh. "Find them. And send him back in pieces." She strolled to the door. "Now."

Nate grabbed her arm as she passed through the

circle of Demons. "What about him?" He nodded to Grier.

Thanks, Nate.

She looked at his hand until he dropped it. "He's with me. And nobody touches him." She took Grier roughly by the arm and tugged. "I'll see everyone in the bar in an hour."

They walked out together, and to her credit, she waited until the shop door swung closed behind them before she threw up on his shoes.

iona dropped the toothbrush into the sink.

Killing a man, being the one to pull the trigger, wasn't as easy as she'd thought it would be, as easy as Max had told her it was. She braced a hand on each side of the vanity top and looked at herself in the mirror. Good hair. Mascara a little smudged, but nothing she couldn't fix. She looked the same as she had before she shot a man in cold blood. Before she'd order him chopped to bits and returned to Willy Carr and Tyler Sedotal.

Grier knocked on the door. She'd left him in the outer office while she cleaned herself up. He walked in and stood behind her, laid his hand on her back and drew her close when she turned into him.

She didn't need to be cradled. Or coddled. Or babied. She needed not to see the life drain out of Kale's eyes when she closed hers. She needed Grier and wrapped her arms around him, slipped one hand under his shirt and used the other to yank him down for a kiss. Not one of those sweet meetings of their mouths. Her need was raw, primal, desperate in ways she'd never been before. Tongues dueling. Breaths huffing. She wanted him to take control of the moment, to tell her to suck his cock then lift her onto the counter and fuck her until she screamed.

She angled her head. More. She needed more of him. Her hands attacked his button fly, and she groped for his dick, wanted to feel it throb in her palm. She jerked her head away. "Tell me to get on my knees, Grier."

He yanked open her shirt, dragged down the cup of her support bra and took her nipple into his mouth.

"Oh, God, Grier."

She pumped his cock, stroked the shaft, and continued to moan until he lifted his head. "Go down on me." He groaned as she took him into her mouth and swirled her tongue over the tip. "Can you see yourself in the mirror? How fucking hot you look with my dick in your mouth?"

She glanced at the full-length mirror on the back of the door as she bobbed her head and his dick slid in and out of her mouth. There was something so erotic about watching herself.

"Touch your pussy." He pulled her to her feet and

spun her so her back was against his chest and she could see herself. "Slide your pants down but leave your panties on." He waited until she kicked off her leggings then laid his hand over hers to slide it down her belly into the waistband of her underwear. His dick settled against the small of her back, and he ground his hips as their hands worked together to tease her.

Her eyes fluttered shut as he used his free hand to flick her nipple until it pebbled hard and he gave a gentle pinch and roll.

"Open your eyes, Fiona. Watch yourself get off." He dipped a finger inside her and her knees went weak. Oh, God. The pressure inside her built, tensing every muscle and cell until he pulled their hands away and lifted her onto the counter then slid into her. There was nothing gentle about the way he took her. Every move caused a moan, an urgency for more. "Watch me fuck you, baby."

And she did. Every thrust, the way he lifted her leg and held it on his shoulder as he plunged in and out of her, as his ass tightened, and he hung onto the counter for leverage.

Her pussy squeezed him, and she cried out as the world burst and she blew apart. "Fiona!" His voice went husky, and his thrusts harder until he shuddered and leaned his forehead against hers. "Jesus."

She closed her eyes. "Thank you."

He chuckled, then coughed as he withdrew. "Anytime." Now here was a man who could make her forget anything and damned if she planned to let him go. Not now anyway. He brushed a finger from her temple to her jaw. "Seriously. Anytime. I don't care what I'm doing. Where I'm at. You call. I'm there."

Even with only one eye open and his face every shade of purple on the color wheel and more than a little swollen, she'd still never seen a more attractive man. "I'll keep it in mind."

He nodded toward the shower. "Shall we? I feel a little dirty." He wiggled his eyebrows.

* * *

FIONA WALKED into the bar calmer than she'd felt in a while. She didn't know a damned thing more than she'd known earlier, but thanks to Grier, she felt more equipped to handle the guys. Grier walked to the bar, and Jez slid him a bottle of beer. At least if no one else believed in Grier, Jez seemed to.

Hamilton, by contrast, glared at Grier, his eyes narrow and his mouth in a thin, grim line. She ignored him and looked around the room. Sage, Jim, Nate, Dale, all the guys waiting for her to explain, to answer their unasked questions, to make Grier's presence acceptable after he'd gone behind their backs to the FBI.

She blew out a breath and smiled. "We have a problem."

"A couple of them apparently." Nate shot a look at Grier. An if-looks-could-kill-Grier'd-be-dead look.

Max wouldn't tolerate interruptions. Never had. And neither would she. And she could shoot her own looks. He shifted in his chair and crossed his arms, but he shut up and that was a win for Fiona. "Okay, so Grier's staying. And I don't have to tell you why. Max wouldn't have and you wouldn't have asked." All true. "But I'm going to." She glanced around the room again. Good. She had their attention. "Dave was FBI. And through the years he was a driver for us, we had a man on the inside, someone who gave us details and helped us skirt around the things that could have taken the club down. No one knew about Dave but Max and Grier. Now we don't have Dave." Sad, but reality. "And we have the FBI beating at our door to take Ham."

Griff stood and turned a wide circle, arms spread. "I don't see the FBI anywhere."

"You didn't see a traitor standing in this room for the last two or three months either." She lifted her chin, a dare for him to defy her further. "Now sit down." She waited until his ass hit wood then she breathed deep and started again. "They think Grier's going to deliver Ham."

Hamilton scoffed. "And you think he won't?"

"I know he won't."

Hamilton needed a minute to get the words out. His fury, what she could see in his red face and stormy eyes, always robbed him of the ability for fast speech and quick thought. "You think leading him around by his dick is going to keep him loyal to a club he lied to? Keep me out of prison?"

She didn't have to glance at Grier to know he was ready for another fight. God, she hoped her kid didn't have that kind of temper. And thank God Grier had told her everything after their shower. She smiled. During, he'd been a little busy.

"You aren't going to prison." She held up the picture of Grier with Dave. "Grier will go before you do. But we have an option that keeps all the Demons outside the cells. Free men. And Grier's conversation with the FBI gave us the intel we need to make it happen."

She told them about the camp, the one her father had built before they'd found the warehouse. As soon as it had come up, she knew, remembered Uncle Willy and the underground tunnels beneath log cabins and the building in the compound.

"You want us to take Carr and Sedotal?"

And there it was. The bloodlust she'd counted on them having. "Not yet. For right now, we watch." She'd been young, really young, when they'd abandoned the camp for the warehouse, but she knew enough to get close to it, maybe even to find a tunnel or two to get inside. But it would take finesse and planning. They couldn't go in guns blazing and knives swinging. Not if they wanted to make it work. They had to be swift and smart. "We need to learn what they're doing and when they plan on doing it."

"How the hell are you going to manage that?" Jim stood and walked to the front. "I say we go in and blow the fuckers up."

"And send Ham or Grier straight to the gas chamber or the electric chair or whatever they do now. These are your brothers."

Jim shook his head. "And we do what we have to do no matter what it costs us personally. They knew it when they came in." He scoffed at her. Smirked even. "Or is your girlie heart not strong enough to watch your little play toy go down on anything but you." He edged forward and Grier and Hamilton both stood. "Who you protecting? The club or that fucking traitor you married?"

He towered over her by a foot and she should have been quaking and scared, but she smiled. "Jim, you were one of my dad's best friends. Since I can remember." She shook her head pretending to be lost in a fond memory before she hardened her face and stared up at him. "But I will shoot you in the face if you question my dedication to these guys and this place and everything my father built. If you don't like what I do," she held her hands out, "then take your shot." She looked away from Jim and out at the rest of the room. "That goes for all of you. But you just know that my dad built this into what it is. He put the money in your pockets and the blow up your noses. And he chose me to get you into the future. To keep you safe and off the fed radar. You don't trust me? Fuck you. Walk. But until one of you is big enough to take my chair, you'll do what I say."

These pregnancy hormones were amazing, gave her courage even. And she would use it to hang onto her position as long as she could.

* * *

Fiona leaned on the bar and stared at him until heat crawled over his skin and he took a long drink from his beer. "What?"

She leaned in and put her arm around his waist to slip her finger through the belt loop on his opposite hip. The warmth of her breath tingled in his ear. "I have this fantasy about you."

And now she had his attention. "Yeah? You want to tell me about it?"

She nodded and rubbed her tits against his arm. His dick twitched. She laced her fingers with his and pulled. "I want to show you."

And because he couldn't have said no if he had

wanted to, he let her lead him out of the bar, through the shop and to the car she'd driven there. "Car sex?"

"Nope." She climbed in the driver's side. "I have to show you something. Take me home."

He drove. She left her hand on his leg, stroking with one finger as he raced the car toward their place. He smiled at the thought. Their place.

There was nothing about Fiona he didn't love. Her beauty, her wit, her charm, the way she'd stood toe to toe with Jim and dared any one of the club to try to remove her as their leader. The fact she carried his baby without complaint, complaints she would have been entitled to make, like swollen ankles, fatigue, whatever aches came along with pregnancy.

He glanced at her, reclined in the seat next to him. "I love you." He wanted to say it, needed her to know he didn't only tell her when it suited his purpose or when it could benefit him somehow.

She smiled. "We'll see in a minute."

He pulled into the driveway and shut off the car. She reached into the glove compartment and pulled out a flashlight then opened the door. "Come on. I have some-thing to show you."

Instead of going to the house, she walked around the side and opened the back gate then clicked the button on the light. A triangle of light in front of her led them to a small garage at the back of the property, a garage he didn't even know belonged to her. She pulled a key from over the doorframe, unlocked the door and pushed it open. Before he could walk through behind her, she stood in the doorway. "Please understand I was angry at you, and I'm sorry."

Oh, God. If she had a body locked in the garage it was going to be a very long night. "I thought this was about your fantasy."

"It is. But first…" She flipped a switch and moved out of the doorway as an overhead light shined down on his bike. Not the spare he'd been riding since she'd brought him back from Belize, but his bike… the one he'd spent hours building under Max's guidance.

She'd told him it was gone. Parted out then burned. "Well, you little liar, you." He couldn't decide whether to be angry or whether he wanted to kiss her. Instead of doing either, he walked inside, closer, mouth hanging open, so damned glad to see his bike he could've cried with joy. "You already told me you had it." A while back even and he'd waited patiently for her to return it. Patient to the point he'd forgotten about it.

"Yeah. But I thought it was time to give it back." She breathed in deep. Aside from the ass kicking and the fact every guy in the club probably still wanted him dead, this had turned out to be a great day.

He watched the uncertainty play across her face.

"Come here." His smile was pretty easy to hide behind the busted lips and bruised face.

Fiona straddled the bike in front of him, her hands on his shoulders, her ass on the gas tank. He leaned in to kiss her gently then drew away. "Now, about that fantasy..." He had a fairly good idea, but waited for her to strip off her shirt, and lean back so her head rested between the handlebars. "On the bike?"

"On it, over it. Since you took me to school that last day senior year, all I could think about was your cock sliding in and out of me while the bike roared underneath us." She sat up and sealed her mouth to his, pulling him forward as she laid back.

Finally, after a lifetime of having nothing, Grier Owen had everything he'd ever wanted. And god damned if he'd let anything come in the way of it.

9

Grier Fucking Owen was taking this pampering his wife thing a bit far. He'd been at her side for weeks. If she shopped, he drove, carried her bags, helped her to the car. When she got her nails done, he read a magazine in the waiting area. If she took a shower, he washed her back. Although, she didn't mind that one so much. But she hadn't had a moment alone since she couldn't remember when and she just needed some time.

Now he stood in her bathroom, waist wrapped in a towel. "What do you think about naming the kid Max?"

Of course she planned to name her son Max. Certainly she wouldn't be naming him Kermit, Grier's actual first name. But that he'd brought it up irrationally irritated her. "*I'll* pick his name when he's born."

Grier shrugged, unbothered by her words or the

tone with which she spat them at him. "I just thought it would be nice to name him after your dad. Or her. It could work for a girl, too."

She jerked her magazine, certain to make sure the rustle of paper was loud enough for him to hear. Then she growled when the page tore and tossed the book onto the foot of the bed. After a quick punch to her pillow, she flopped down and closed her eyes. Hopefully, he would take the hint.

"To be honest, I promised Max before he died."

He promised Max. Her father. "Well, you didn't have the right."

He put his razor down and walked out of the bathroom to sit next to her on the bed. He still had shaving cream on half of his face. "I'm sorry, Fiona. I just wanted to give him a little joy in however long he had left." He brushed her hair off her face and let his hand linger on her back.

And now she felt like a shit. Again, Grier's fault. She couldn't tell if the anger was from the hormones or because he'd really pissed her off. And she couldn't figure it out with him hovering. "I haven't been sleeping well. I can't get comfortable with you in here."

What? The only time she was comfortable was tucked into his side with her leg over his.

"I can sleep on the sofa." She didn't miss the flash of

hurt in his eyes as he stood and went back to the bathroom to finish shaving.

Shit. "Don't bother. I won't be able to sleep anyway. I've got too much on my mind." Grier's fault.

He hung the towel on the hook and walked out of the bathroom to pull a pair of boxers from the drawer in his dresser. The one that made her room too crowded. She'd had to move her reading chair into the living room. Grier's fault.

A month ago, this man in his underwear would have had her ripping her own clothes off to get to him, but now, it annoyed her. She'd bought him twenty pairs of pajama pants that were dry rotting on a shelf in the closet. She huffed out a sigh. "What's wrong?"

She sat up and twisted to face him. "I bought you pajamas. You think you could wear them, just once maybe, so it isn't a total waste of money?"

"Sure."

And really, did he have to be so agreeable. About every damned thing? He came back out of the closet, a ridiculous pair of plaid pants riding low on his hips. "Better?" He turned in a circle so she could see.

"Don't mock me."

He held up both hands. "I'm not." He slid onto the bed and she turned toward the window. "Hey, are you mad at me?" Even the softness of his voice grated on her.

"No." And yes. And no again. She hated this. She

hated not feeling like herself or being able to control her body. And now, her eyes welled with tears. Fuck. "I don't like being pregnant." Her voice came in a whiny whimper she also hated.

He laid a hand on her shoulder. "What can I do to help you?"

She turned and looked up at him, didn't turn away when he brushed a thumb across her cheek to catch a tear. "Nothing. I'm big and fat and I pee when I sneeze. I cried today when Jim brought me the mail. Not because there was anything in the mail but a circular, but because he thought to bring it to me. And my pants don't fit." Dear God. Where had all this come from and why couldn't she make it stop. Words poured out of her. "I don't want to pee when I sneeze, Grier. I don't want to be shaped like a traffic cone, and I'm tired of crying all the time, and I don't want to lose you because I'm being mean."

She sniffed and sobbed into his shoulder. His arms came around her and he held her until the tears dried up and she could finally get a hold of herself.

"Better?" When she nodded, he smiled. "A couple of things… you're not shaped like a traffic cone. There is nothing you could do to lose me, and… well, I don't really know what to say about the sneezing."

She chuckled. "Can I tell you one more thing?"

He kissed her forehead. "You can tell me anything."

This wasn't fair. She wanted to be normal again, to enjoy her husband, to fit into her own clothes. "I need a few minutes every day without you in it. I'm dying here. Everywhere I go, you're always there. I mean, you haven't been out riding since that first night when I gave your bike back. And I love being with you." She snuggled closer, hoping he could feel how important he was to her. "But I need to breathe."

He kissed the top of her head and held her tighter. "There are men out there ready to hurt you. I can't take that chance. I won't."

His heartbeat under her ear lulled her raging hormones into a peaceful bliss. "I know, but I can't be watched all the time. I promise. I'll be careful, I'll be diligent and I'll take someone with me if I go away from the shop, but you sitting in my office all day, reading me Facebook funnies and showing me Instagram pics..." She sighed. "We're spending too much time together."

He snored softly in her ear.

"Jerk."

* * *

GRIER WATCHED THE COMPOUND, Sage on his right, and Jim, a hundred yards away, on his left. They'd stowed their bikes in the trees and walked in. So far, they'd seen no movement, no sign anyone had ever been inside the compound.

Sage smiled down at his phone, typed in a few words then shoved it into his pocket. He looked over at Grier. "Haven't seen you out in a while. You get tired of carrying Fiona's shopping bags?"

Grier would have carried her bags until his arms fell off, but he damned sure wasn't going to admit it to Sage. Not even to Kye. "Nah. She got tired of me."

"Honeymoon's over, huh?" Sage chuckled.

After yet another fight at breakfast, well, Fiona had fought, he'd bit his tongue and remained silent, he'd decided to leave her with Hamilton for the day. She was carrying his baby. The least he could do was let her get her anger out. Even if she did it at a decibel that threatened his normal hearing functions.

"Yeah. I guess."

Sage picked up the binoculars and stared at one of the cottages. "What do you think they have in there?"

Hmm. Grier hadn't considered where they might have stored the shipments they'd stolen from the Demons. But certainly, seven shipments would fit inside the ten or so cottages. And now, he wanted to know. He slid through the brush where they'd made their surveillance spot. There were plenty of trees and shrubs to hide behind as he pushed closer until he could reach out and touch the cottage.

The windows were low enough he would only need to stand straight to look inside, but a rustling behind him forced him face down next to the cabin. Sage tapped his shoulder. "You startle easy."

Grier narrowed his eyes and glared. "Shut up."

"What's in there?" Sage stage-whispered the question.

"I don't know. I was about to look when you came up." And now Jim joined them, clomping through the crunching leaves at his full-height. No 007 in their game.

Sage pulled Jim's arm so he crouched beside them. "You look. We'll watch your back."

Grier nodded and stood. Stacks of boxes lined the walls and he would have bet his life every single box belonged to the Screaming Demons.

He squatted. "FBI has been all over this place. How'd they get those boxes in here?" Damned if he would leave before he knew. "Watch the road and the doors." He didn't wait for an answer but pressed his back against the wall and slid across the cedar logs to the front of the cottage. Certainly they wouldn't leave the door unlocked, but when he tried the knob—no point in breaking in if he didn't have to—it twisted and the latch worked free.

Stupid fuckers. Or it was a trap. Too late to just close the door now. He walked inside, keeping his head below the window line. The boxes made a maze into the room and he stepped carefully around. "I'll be damned." A hatch in the floor was open, a ladder below.

He stood back when voices from below floated up. Grier recognized Demuer's voice. "They're protecting him now, but I did what you asked and I want my money."

Another voice laughed. "Your money? You haven't earned shit." Grier would've recognized that voice in his sleep. Tyler Sedotal. And as much as he wanted to go down there and rip him limb from fucking limb, he stood still, concealed behind the boxes. "That cock-sucker is out there still, not in prison, not dead. You get me Grier Owen's head and you'll get your money. Simple as that." Heavy footsteps echoed away.

They—and he wasn't quite sure who *they* were yet—weren't after Fiona at all. Interesting. This had been a very *interesting* endeavor.

Grier wanted to know what was under this cottage. Boy, did he want to know. He moved around the stack he was hiding behind, misjudged the amount of space his body took in a crouched position and the pile teetered, wobbled, swayed, and crashed to the ground. Grier made for the door. Left it flopping open and ran for the woods, Sage and Jim following as the first shots rang out.

They ran for their bikes, with Sage returning fire

over his shoulder and Jim stumbling through the brush. Sage climbed on his bike and gunned the engine into a full turn as Jim took a bullet in the leg. Grier grabbed him under his arm and half-dragged him to his bike. "Get on!"

Shots rained around them, pinging off trees, ricocheting around them and Grier sped away.

Fuck. He'd destroyed any chance he had of catching Sedotal in his lair. And that wasn't something he wanted to have to tell Fiona.

* * *

BY DARK, the cottages were surrounded by Screaming Demons. Fiona had taken the details better than he'd expected. "Get our stuff back." That was all she'd said, but her slumped shoulders and the weariness in her eyes let him know he'd disappointed her.

They'd left her Hamilton and Jim, then every available man and Jez loaded into the trucks with their bikes and enough weaponry to bring down a small country. One by one they emptied the cottages and retrieved every damned thing that had been stolen with the exception of the truck that had burned and was still in police custody.

For being watched by the FBI, a lie that led Grier to believe the three agents he'd met with were all dirty, the cottages were unprotected and unlocked. And something about it didn't feel right.

He walked out to the last truck and opened one of the boxes. Nothing but parts and pills. He pushed the box away and closed the sliding door. He still wanted to see what was in the basement, but not now. He had to get these trucks to safety. Fiona was counting on him and he'd let her down enough for one day.

"Let's go." He climbed on his bike and took the lead with Sage. Demons rode between and beside each truck and the devastation wouldn't have been so total had he checked more than one box, had he thought the way Tyler Sedotal thought.

The first truck exploded, and Nate swerved off the road, laying the bike on its side in the grass at the side of the highway. Joe hadn't been so lucky, and rider and bike had slid under the burning truck in a slick of oil and sparks. Every truck took out one rider and left two. Cargo littered the streets, rocketed up then crashed back down. Bodies of his men, brothers, Demons, laid in pieces amid flames and heat. The cops would be on their asses over the stolen parts and the drugs, the explosions, and the dead bodies they didn't have time to retrieve.

And every bit of it was Grier's fault.

For all of her education, all of her life experience as of late, Fiona couldn't figure out how to console Grier. He hadn't moved off the sofa in days. Hadn't showered. Hadn't eaten much either. She'd dealt with funeral planning, police questions, and the hospital, and he had stayed curled on the sofa. Stoic. Silent. Possibly catatonic. In a t-shirt and basketball shorts.

Out of desperation, she'd called Sage. And Jez. And Hamilton. They all stood in her kitchen, huddled together watching Grier. Jez peeking around Hamilton, waving her hands at Grier in a wax-on-wax-off motion. He didn't so much as glance up.

"He's like a bad throw rug."

Fiona rolled her eyes. "Jez, be helpful."

Sage sighed. "I'll go." His arm was wrapped in a white

bandage where a radiator full of black-market boner pills had come down and cut him open from elbow to wrist, but he'd stuck around, bleeding and faint, to help with the bodies of the fallen brothers. He walked into the kitchen and sat on the coffee table in front of Grier. Grier didn't move or even look up. He sat for a minute without speaking then stood and slid his hands down his pants legs. He walked back to join the huddle in the kitchen.

"He's a lump." Sage shrugged.

Could she possibly have picked less helpful people to fix this? "He couldn't have checked every box. There wasn't enough time. You guys didn't know what was waiting for you out there." Fiona had said the very same words to Grier and still nothing. No reaction.

Jez stared at him. "Has he eaten?"

"Not in a while." Fiona was failing Wife 101. She couldn't even get her husband to open his mouth and put food in it.

"All right. I'll go to the store and stock up."

Hamilton dropped a hand on Fiona's shoulder. "I'm going in, but I hope you know, I'm only doing this for you." He ducked through the doorway and made his way to the same spot Sage had sat. "It's not your fault."

When Grier failed to move, he looked at Fiona, and she widened her eyes, twirling her hands in the universal sign for keep going. She'd tried everything already and wouldn't blame Hamilton if he gave up, but he sighed and turned back to Grier. If he could fix her husband, Fiona was going to owe him so big.

"You should've checked the boxes. True. And the guys wouldn't be dead if you did. Also true." He shook his head and squeezed Grier's shoulder in one meaty hand. "You were the guy in charge. It's on you."

What the hell? "Hamilton." But he held up his hand, and she stayed in her spot. She put her fist against her mouth, closed her eyes and hoped he had a direction he was heading.

"And every man followed you, knowing the danger, because they wanted to be there. They followed you, Grier, and no one is questioning you now." Hamilton chuckled a little. "Shit like this happens in our line of work. It's part of who we are. We take risks that could end us anytime. And those guys died to be Demons. They died for you and for what they believed was the right thing. Not a damned one of them had to go with you that night." He cleared his throat, and Fiona wondered if he was choked up or thirsty. Probably thirsty. Hamilton wasn't the kind of guy who let his emotions run with him. "And you lying here wallowing is not how we need to be honoring our brothers."

Good one. She hadn't thought to use guilt.

"What do you expect me to do? I killed them."

She hadn't heard his voice in days and now it washed

over her and apparently the baby who kicked her in her ribs. She put a hand over the spot.

"No, this was a job that went wrong. Jobs do that." Fiona had never seen Hamilton so gentle, so soft. "We can't fix this, Grier, but we can make sure nothing happens to Fiona and the baby, that the guys who died get their justice. Demon justice."

Grier glanced up. He needed to shave, kind of. The shadow of beard was sexy enough, Fiona could get used to it. It would take hours of conditioner to get the knots out of his hair, but to Fiona, he'd never looked better. He scrubbed his hands over his face. "How?" He wasn't asking Hamilton, but Fiona.

The plan wasn't set yet. Not even close. They'd kicked around ideas, but without good intel, and they had none, beyond sitting in the clubhouse, cleaning guns, loading clips, and spending a lot of time at target practice, there wasn't anything they could set in concrete. Plus, the cops were around a lot now. They'd hauled everyone from Fiona to the lowliest Wall Kat in for questioning. But when the Screaming Demons put up a wall of silence, it was impenetrable. Thank God.

The money they were spending in lawyer fees was enough to break them when it went along with the missing shipments that had gone up in flames, the replacement trucks, and funeral expenses. Fiona didn't know what she'd do if she lost one of her guys, or Grier, to jail.

"I don't know, yet." She crossed into the living room, her throat thick and her eyes wet. "But we can't do it without you. We can't…" She sat beside him and put her head on his shoulder, hoping the shift in his body wasn't him trying to shake her off.

Her smile, for Hamilton, was shrouded in tears, and he nodded at her before he turned to Grier. "When you're ready, hopefully soon, we need you back. We need to work out what to do."

Grier nodded. "I'm ready."

The cocked eyebrow, half-smirk, and slight offset of his head was the most expression Hamilton ever put forth. "Maybe shower first. Do something with that girlie hair of yours, then you'll be ready." When Grier nodded, Hamilton winked at Fiona. "And when you come in, don't worry. We all have your back." He held out his hand. "Brother."

Grier nodded and shook Hamilton's hand. "Thanks."

Emotions she hadn't let touch her since this all began caught Fiona's breath and brought tears, as she nestled closer to Grier. For the first time, she allowed herself to acknowledge that it could've been him who had died, could've been him whose body she had to identify. These last few days, when he'd been caught up in his feelings, she'd kept hers locked down, but the sadness and loneliness had always been like a little gnat, flittering at the back of her mind. But imagining him gone, out of reach where she couldn't even look at him, forced a lump into her throat, and a sob shook her shoulders. The guys who'd died had been friends, men she'd grown up around or ones who'd come later, guys who relied on her father then her to make sure they had money, and booze, and a measure of safety and brotherhood. She felt their loss, and it hurt, but losing Grier would kill. Even if he wouldn't or couldn't comfort her now.

She put her arm across his stomach and buried her head in the curve of his shoulder.

"I love you." He didn't hug her or even acknowledge the words, but she felt better for saying them.

He pushed off the blanket and stood. "I should go get cleaned up."

Fiona watched him walk away, hoping her husband was back, knowing he wasn't.

GRIER LEANED his forehead against the wall and let the water rush over him. At least the sobbing had subsided. Of course, so had the hot water.

"Can I come in?"

Ordinarily, before, he would have been happy to let Fiona join him, but now, knowing how badly he'd let everyone down, he just wanted to be alone. "I'll be out in a second."

"Okay. Um, well, Jez made lunch and if you don't come out and eat, she's threatening to have Hamilton try to force-feed you so… um, hurry, okay?" He'd put the uncertainty in her voice, made her doubt him and it was killing him. And probably her. The best thing he could do would be to leave, let her find someone else. The thought of not coming home to her, not having her to hold, made his heart ache, but what else could he do? If he left, Sedotal would come after him, would leave her alone. Everyone, Fiona, Jez, the club, would be safer without Grier bringing all this death and destruction that seemed to be following him.

"Yeah."

Grier shut the water off and toweled dry then dressed in jeans a little looser than before and a t-shirt that hung longer on his frame. As he pulled on his socks, he heard the sound of the first explosion. The sound he'd been hearing in his head since that day. He didn't even have to close his eyes and there it was. When he breathed, he could still smell the smoke and feel the heat of the flames as he and Sage tried to save whoever they could get to. Fuck. Would it never end?

His stomach rolled, and he dashed back to the bathroom. He couldn't do this. Couldn't walk around pretending this wasn't his fault. He wiped his mouth with the back of his hand then sat on the floor against the wall. He might've sat there for an hour or a week, probably just a few minutes, but he couldn't bring himself to stand, couldn't walk out there and face all the people he'd let down.

At the knock on the door, he looked up but didn't move until it pushed open. "Hey."

Jez walked in and shut the door behind her. She sat down next to him and took his hand. "I know you're in a bad place in your head. It hurts, but you're not the only one hurting. And she doesn't have a choice about getting up and going on. She doesn't get to curl up on the couch and cry even though it's probably what she needs to do. These were her friends, too. *Our* friends. And she's dealing with the cops, the customers, the club, and she's pregnant."

"I saw them die." And he couldn't shake the images in his head.

"I know." She shook her head. "And I don't care. I care about her. I care that right now, she's struggling, and the only person she wants to hold her up is you, and you're letting her down." The sternness in her voice added to his guilt. "I think you have to ask yourself what makes you so special that you get to sit here and act like this only happened to you when we all lost those boys."

Everything they'd said today made sense, made him

feel like an epic asshole, but what his head knew and what his body could handle were very different things.

"I watched Griff die." And goddammit, he was crying again.

"I know, baby."

"I couldn't do anything for any of them."

"No, you couldn't. But there's a woman out there who needs you now, and you *can* help her. But if this is the thing that's gonna break you, you don't deserve her because she's held everybody up, and she needs someone strong enough to help her get through this, too."

Grier ran his hand over his face. "I just need a minute."

Jez nodded and stood then held out her hand to help him up. "You've had enough minutes. Either go out there and be the man she needs you to be, or I swear to God and every single man woman and child on this earth, I will shoot you myself."

He didn't doubt she would, he just didn't know if he had anything left in him. "How?"

"With a gun." She wrinkled her eyebrows.

He chuckled. Classic Jez. "I meant—"

"I know what you meant, and I don't care how you do it. If you have to cry in the shower or go for a walk or a ride or whatever, but you be there for her because she would put her shit aside for you, and you damned well know it. She deserves a man who will do the same for her." She pulled her hand to punch it to her hip. "Now, are you gonna get up and be a man or do I go get my gun?"

He stood because he wanted to as much as she hadn't left him a choice. "You're a hard woman, Jez."

She nodded. "You don't last as long as I do without picking up a little grit." She opened the door and frowned at the squeak of the hinges. "A little cooking oil on that hinge will fix that."

Apparently being around this long also gave her a bit of DIY knowledge, too. However, she'd also managed to point out just one more way he'd failed as a husband.

"I'll get on it." As soon as he made the last few days up to Fiona. And that started with an apology.

He followed Jez into the kitchen where Fiona stood at the counter with her back to them. When she turned, he put his arms around her and drew her close. "I'm sorry."

Instead of speaking, she laid her head over his heart and breathed out a long sigh. "It's okay." She tilted her chin up and stared into his eyes. "We're gonna get through this. And we're going to figure out what to do to let the world know the Screaming Demons own this town and we're still in charge here."

He nodded. When she said it, he could almost believe it.

iona's medical knowledge could have probably left a thimble half full if she tried to pour it all into one, but she knew they didn't call you into the office to deliver good news. And no amount of comfort or consolation, not that she had any, would make it better. Grier had found a reason, checking out the compound where they'd found their merchandise, not to attend any of her last seven baby appointments. Honestly, how much checking could he do, and did he always have to do it on doctor days?

She sat forward, the weight of her belly these days making her too top-heavy for her back to offer much support. The clock ticked loudly on the wall across from her and the antiseptic smell in the room, or maybe her nerves, incited her nausea, but she closed her eyes and tried to center herself.

Christ. How long could they keep her waiting? Her phone dinged and she pulled it from her pocket, hoping he'd at least thought enough to send her a text. But it was just one from Jez. Three single question marks.

Fiona typed a reply—*still waiting*—and set her phone on the counter as the doctor swung the door open and walked in. Doctor Rutledge was a nice woman, young, smart, and no-nonsense, with shiny blonde hair she let hang down her back and kind eyes.

"Fiona. Good to see you." She held a file folder open in her hand and flipped to a second page as she sat on a rolling chair at the counter.

"Yeah. I wish I could say the same."

The doctor nodded and slapped the folder closed. She looked at Fiona. "Your blood work shows… an abnormality in the baby's chromosomes."

"What does that mean?" Abnormality?

"Down Syndrome is a possibility and…" The doctor paused. "What I want to do is send you for an amniocentesis." She went on to explain the procedure and how it would work. Something about a needle, fluid… risk to the baby was minimal, but present.

"So there's something wrong with my baby?" She put a protective hand over her stomach.

"No." She held up both hands and gave Fiona a soft look that didn't stop the tears from falling.

"Is there someone we can call? Someone who can be

with you during the test?" The doctor laid a hand on Fiona's shoulder.

Fiona blew out a breath. She could do this. She didn't need anyone to be with her. Especially not someone who would rather not be with her. The doctor offered a tissue, and Fiona dried her eyes. "No. I don't want anyone here. But thank you."

"Okay. Well, we're going to go over to the hospital, have you get ready. The test is pretty quick. It's a little uncomfortable."

And holy mother of God was that an understatement. The needle was enormous and the results wouldn't be back for two or three days so that meant she would wait and wonder and probably drive herself crazy, but for now, she was strong and that counted.

As she drove home, she concentrated on the radio, on whatever Bon Jovi song she found on her iPod right up to the minute she pulled into the driveway. Grier's bike was in the open garage and he squatted next to it, wrench in one hand and a streak of grease across his forehead. He stood and smiled as she walked past.

"How'd it go?"

"Fine." She breathed out with the lie.

"Good."

They hadn't found a way to be back to normal since the explosion. They were more like roommates now. Him on the sofa. Her in the bedroom. They ate together.

That was all. But he came home every night and that counted for something.

"I'm going to make supper." She walked into the house and went straight to her room. Sat on the bed and stared at the carpet. After a while, she laid down and closed her eyes.

The room was cloaked in darkness when Grier woke her. "Hey. You okay?"

She put a hand over her belly, wishing she could reach in and hold her baby now. "Yeah. Just tired I guess."

He didn't sit beside her or touch her whatsoever. "I made supper, some BLTs, extra L and T. The way you like."

"Thanks." But she wasn't hungry, wasn't interested in more than those damned three-day test results. "I'll be in there in a few minutes. I just want to wake up a little."

"All right." He walked to the door but turned. "You sure you're okay?"

"Yeah. I'm great." But her breath hitched, and he came back. All she wanted was to be held and soothed, told everything would work out. And she supposed she should tell him, even if he hadn't shown one iota of interest in her or the baby in weeks.

"Fiona?" Now he sat beside her, not touching her, but there and it helped. Sadly. Ridiculously. It helped.

"There might be something wrong with the baby."

Blurting the words made the abstract idea she'd convinced herself it was to be real. And now she couldn't help but think of it. She told him what the doctor said, about the amnio, and that they'd have to wait for the results.

"What do we do?"

She shrugged. "I don't know. Wait, I guess. What choice do we have?" Other than the few tears she'd shed in the doctor's office, she hadn't cried or thought or worked through anything. And now wasn't the time either. She sat up. "Let's go eat."

Because he didn't move, she scooted off the other side of the bed and walked out.

As she set about the ridiculously normal task of putting her sandwich together on her plate, Grier walked in and hugged her from behind. "I'm sorry I wasn't there for you."

She shrugged him off and carried her food to the table. "It's fine."

But it wasn't.

He took her plate and set it in the sink. "Come on."

"What the hell are you doing?" She stood and her nostrils flared when he stood between her and her plate. "I'm hungry. I have a baby to feed."

He nodded and smiled. "Yes. And tonight, we're feeding him something better than greasy sandwiches and iced tea."

Too little. Too late. "Grier, I want my greasy sandwich and my iced tea, and I want to go to bed. Please." There was a bite to her tone that must have swayed him because he set her plate in front of her.

He sat across from her. "I don't know what to do here, Fi. I want to help, to make up for—" he looked down, "—not being there today. Tell me what to do."

She stared at him, saw the fear in his eyes, the worry, the pain. And she closed her eyes. "There's nothing we can do. We just have to wait."

He nodded and scooted his chair closer to hers then took her face in his hands. "I keep messing this up, but I'm gonna be here, beside you. No matter what. Good or bad."

He had his arms around her and held her. And for the first time in a long time, she felt home.

* * *

THE LONGEST THREE days of his life. He'd spent every moment with Fiona, absorbing every emotion she let loose on him, mostly anger, but enough sadness mixed in and he couldn't do much more than worry and try to soothe her. Not that she'd been very receptive to the idea. More than once, she'd pushed him away and he worried about the wall she was building between them. Not that he hadn't played his part, but it still hurt to have her so close and so far away.

Now he waited as she spoke quietly to the doctor on the phone. "Okay… okay… thank you." She hung up and turned to him. "Baby's fine." A slow smile spread across her face as she threw her arms around him and wet his throat with her tears. "She's fine."

"She?" A daughter or hope for a daughter?

"It's a girl." The elation in her voice made him laugh.

"A girl." And when Fiona looked up at him, nothing else in the world mattered but his family. He kissed her cheek first, felt her soft skin under his lips and lingered before he moved down the line of her jaw, around to her chin and to her mouth. Oh, God. He hadn't kissed her in weeks, months and while every kiss had felt new and exciting before, this one was better, familiar, and perfect, and a hundred-percent Fiona.

She kissed him like a woman starving for affection, like someone who needed to be touched and held and loved. She pulled back and stared up at him as she lifted his shirt and pushed it up until he grabbed the collar and yanked it over his head. Then she sealed their lips together, pressured his mouth open with her tongue and let it dance with his while her hands explored his skin.

There were a hundred things he wanted to say, that he needed her to know, but the exquisiteness of her kisses, of her body pressed against his, of the whimpers in her throat, kept him quiet in the moment with her. Needing her. Wanting her.

He swung her into his arms, never breaking the kiss, and carried her to the bedroom. He hadn't slept with her in… too long. Much too long. And she had on so many clothes; a sweater he dispensed with quickly, a shirt underneath that he took his time unbuttoning, kissing every inch of newly revealed skin, an ugly tan bra he was happy to see go, pants with a drawstring that made him ridiculously happy, and a pair of underwear that on anyone else would look ridiculous, but on Fiona made his dick hard enough to mine diamonds.

Fuck, he wanted her, in every way imaginable. He kissed her nipple, swirled his tongue until the nub hardened then sucked it into his mouth. When she gasped, he tried to pull away, but she held his head with her hands tangled in his hair. And he'd never been happier to be held.

"Oh, Grier," she sighed his name, and he lifted his head. "No, please don't stop."

He smiled and kissed her softly on the side of her mouth. "Oh, I'm not stopping." She'd be lucky if he let her out of bed at all the rest of the day. "I just want to look at my beautiful wife."

He ran a hand over her rounded stomach and let it settle just over her belly button. "And our perfect baby."

She pinched her lips together. "You are going to have

to work on your dirty talk." She pushed him onto his back and climbed on top of him. "Talking about the baby right now isn't a big turn on." Her fingers slipped the top button of his pants free but from his view, it looked a lot more seductive than opening a button. "What I'd like to talk about is what I plan to do to my husband to make him smile."

"Ooh. I like that subject." He liked more that she pushed his hands over his head and held them there as she nibbled his lower lip.

"Yeah?" She climbed off him.

"Don't like that." He reached for her and she slapped his hands away. "Come back." Being desperate and horny made his voice an octave higher.

"I will. Just be patient." Her fingers made short work of the buttons to his pants then his boxers. "Now that is how I like to see you."

"Hard?"

"Oh yeah. And naked. You should definitely be hard and naked more." She walked across the room to her dresser and opened a drawer, whatever she withdrew hidden behind her back, then came back to stand beside the bed.

"Trust me, I'm hard most of the time I'm with you." Even recently, when he hadn't felt worthy of her, he'd not been able to control his reaction to having her so near.

She smiled and the room got brighter. "You should mention it. I could help with that."

"I'll make a note." She sat beside him and pulled a scarf from behind her back.

"I have let you be in charge…" She paused and smiled as she slid the silk between her hands. "*Loved* you being in charge, but tonight, I want to be the one who makes the rules. And I want you to lay back and let me." She tied the scarf through the spindled headboard and lifted his arm to wrap the other end around his wrist.

Oh, God. This was… his dick jumped.

Instead of climbing over him, she stood and walked around the bed, trailing another scarf between her tits. He'd be lucky to last another minute. Before he let her have his arm, he pulled her down for another kiss. "All right."

When his wrists were tied, though loose enough he could've worked free, she ran her nail from his collarbone down through the light patch of his chest hair, stopping to circle his nipples, then to his stomach, just before she touched the dripping head of his cock. He moaned when she lightly bit his nipple then held it between her teeth to give it a little twist. "Fiona. God."

"Shh." This time she raked her fingers up the inside of his thigh as she moved to the other nipple. If she kept this up, no way would he make it long enough to please her.

He wanted to touch her, make her cry out his name, make her come until her knees buckled and her eyes crossed and she fell asleep in his arms.

"Close your eyes, Grier."

"I want to see."

She moved away from the bed, back to the dresser. "And I want you to close your eyes. Hmm. What should we do?" She pulled out another scarf and waved it at him.

No. No. No. At least if he closed his eyes, he could possibly sneak a few glances. "You win."

When his eyelids closed, he listened for the tread of her feet against the carpet, the rustle of the blanket, anything that would tell him she'd come back. "No peeking."

She ran the silk along the same path her finger had taken but instead of his nipples, she let it drag over the head of his dick. He sucked in a breath and bit his lower lip. The bed dipped next to him and she ran her foot over his calf to his knee and back down. "I really like looking at you."

"And I would like to look at you." Everywhere she touched, burned, but he wanted her to enjoy this, to feel his surrender to her. Not that he wouldn't peek, given the chance.

"Are you talking again? There's a penalty." She let her

roaming hand slip along his hip on the opposite side. "Do you want a penalty, Grier?"

He shook his head.

"Good." She kissed him hard, bit his lower lip, and sucked his tongue into her mouth. He felt every pull deep in his gut. "Did you know…" She straddled his cock and put her hand on his chest, curling her fingers into his chest hair. "I have been dreaming about this since that day in the mall?" She lifted her hips and leaned forward so that her nipple grazed his mouth. He flicked it with his tongue, and she moaned. The sound went straight from his ear canal south. "It's why I told Daddy you were the one I wanted to marry." She kissed him again. "And kind of because you did me so wrong, I wanted to punish you."

What? He tested the knot holding him to the bed, found it loose still, and relaxed.

"I'm not going to now. You've more than made up for leaving me there with my pussy wet and half the store hearing me get myself off because you wouldn't."

Oh, God. He remembered that day. The little black scrap of fabric that didn't cover near enough skin for his dick not to get noticed. And the way she'd pushed her body into his, forced him against the wall. He wanted to ask if she'd finished for him, but he concentrated on not shooting a load all over himself instead. A couple of deep breaths and he was back under control.

Her thighs squeezed his hips as she rocked up then took his dick in her hand and stroked him. She'd probably twisted her torso around enough he could take a quick look, but he didn't risk it yet. She wouldn't be able to keep this up much longer, wouldn't be able to continue teasing him, without taking some pleasure for herself. At least he hoped not.

"Do you know what I really want?"

He shook his head again.

"I want you to taste me." She ran a damp finger over his lips, and he licked the salty, sweetness that was the very essence of her until she drew away. "Do you want more?"

He wanted everything. He nodded.

"Then ask me." The confidence in her tone was almost as hot as the way she touched him.

He would have walked through a plate-glass window if she asked him to. "Can I have more?" He added, "Please."

"Do you want to lick me?"

"God, yes. Please." Begging wasn't beneath him.

She stopped stroking him and turned so her pussy hovered over his face and her ass was in the air above him. Now this was a view worth risking the penalty for open eyes.

When her mouth wrapped around the shaft of his dick, he lifted his head and ran his tongue from her clit to the opening of her pussy. Oh, God. She was every-thing. The entire world.

Her mouth moved over him, taking all of him in then her tongue slicked over the head as she bobbed up, and he thrust his tongue inside her. The whimper in her throat vibrated his dick, and he pulled his arm free to wrap around her leg, holding her there in case she tried to get away.

She concentrated her efforts, amazing efforts, on the sweet spot that lit his world up and his balls tightened. He dug his fingers into her skin and continued licking her even as he came until her legs clenched and she cried out and rocked against him.

When she climbed off, he pulled his still-tied arm free and settled her into his side. "That was… amazing."

"I enjoyed it." She turned her face to press a kiss against his chest. "And as much as I want to keep going, I'm so tired, Grier."

"We have time." He pulled the bottom corner of the blanket over them and fell asleep with his wife for the first time in a long time.

12

Once upon a time, Fiona was young and naïve and believed the world couldn't touch her. She'd grown up a lot since then. And since things were going so well with Grier, even with the club, though they still hadn't managed to track down Sedotal or discover why he'd targeted the Demons, a tightening in her stomach warned her things were about to fall apart. Or maybe it was labor. She still had three weeks to go, but the time couldn't pass quickly enough and every rumble, gas bubble, and hiccup instilled a new bout of hope that she would be meeting her baby that day. Of course, so far it had never happened.

Hamilton poked his head in her office. "You doing okay?"

Oh, and the number of random visitors to her office asking if she was *doing okay* had increased by the thousands. Probably not thousands per se, but it felt like it. She nodded. "Just waddling along."

Hamilton walked in and shut the door behind him. That meant a serious discussion, likely about something she didn't want to know about. She waited until he took the seat across from her.

"What's up?"

"Kye's in town."

Well, wasn't that something? Kye Driscoll. And Fiona had no idea how she felt about it. He'd turned traitor, convinced Grier to go rogue against the club, then somehow ended up in Belize on the island she'd forced Grier to leave. She folded her hands over her belly. "What's he doing here?"

"Don't know."

"The lawyer bitch come back with him?" Not that she knew Eliana well, but the family history there wasn't something Fiona could forget. Her dad skimmed money, screwed the club, made side deals, then had the audacity to wither and die before he could take his revenge.

"No. He came in on a commercial flight. Got here at noon. Been sitting down Hell Hollow road since." Sitting on the road leading straight to the clubhouse. Interesting. Hamilton spoke in a monotone which meant absolutely nothing since he usually did. But the darkness in his eyes, the fury she had the power to let loose burned behind the black expression. "You want me to get him?"

Did she? And what would she do with him if she did? "Yeah." And shamefully, the doubt she'd had about her husband sneaked back in. "And bring Grier with you." He'd passed every test she put in front of him, done every single thing she'd asked, and still... she couldn't be sure he would choose her.

Hamilton stood and left, and now she had nothing to do but wait and find out.

* * *

KYE SLOUCHED in front of her desk, as handsome as he'd ever been but darker tan than she remembered from even the last time she saw him on the island when she'd gone to retrieve Grier.

Grier stood next to him on one side and Hamilton on the other. "Good to be back?"

His eyes crinkled at the corners from all that sun damage when he smiled. "I always liked it here." He glanced around. "A little different than I remember."

"I made some improvements." In Max's day—the thought of her father made her heart ache—the office had been more masculine, minus the crystal chandelier, the white fur rug, the white leather chairs and the small settee with pristine snowy fur trim.

He glanced at her bulging stomach. "And some expansions. Congratulations."

"It's a girl."

"I just had a boy."

She knew it already. Grier had felt it necessary to tell her. "Congratulations to you then."

Nothing about Kye had changed. He was still cocky, smoother than chocolate pudding. He looked over his shoulder at the chair. "You mind?" When she shrugged, he pulled the chair up to his side of her desk and plopped into the seat. "We need to talk."

"Well, I didn't bring you here for entertainment." That he was so comfortable, so entitled, burned in her gut. He'd walked away from all this for a woman. And while she might have understood it, she had to make sure he knew she didn't condone it. He didn't speak, just raised his eyebrows as if waiting for her to make another move in their pathetic little game of, not chess, but tic-tac-toe. She glanced at Grier and Hamilton. "Could you guys give us a second? But stay close."

"We'll be outside the door." Hamilton turned and Grier's mouth dropped open.

Apparently, her husband didn't like being dismissed. "Fiona."

She cocked her head to the side and stared at him. It was one thing to lead a few meetings, to collect rents and to take control in their bedroom but questioning her in front of Kye was wrong. "Go."

He glared for a moment, then turned and stalked out.

When the door slammed behind him, Fiona sat back in her chair. "I'm tired, Kye, and I don't feel like playing right now. So if you could just tell me why you're here, I'll probably hate you a little bit less."

He chuckled. "I like that you're very direct. Your honesty's always been one of the best things about you." She shot him a withering glance. He didn't wither. But he held up a hand. "Fine. Grier's in trouble."

Why the fuck did Kye have intel she didn't? She lived with Grier, slept with him every night, and he hadn't mentioned one damned thing. If he'd told Kye and not her... "What does *in trouble* mean?" Oh, God. Please nothing that the club would hate him for. She couldn't go ten rounds with each of the guys over him. Not now.

He shrugged. "I don't know exactly. All I know is a rough biker type showed up in Belize asking around about him."

"You used to be a rough biker type. Now you look like you'd rather ride a wave than a Harley." Grier had looked the same when she'd brought him back and she would have smiled at the memory but a stab of electricity shot through her stomach. Instead of speaking further, she opened the drawer for the folder where she stored the mug shots of Tyler Sedotal and Willy Carr she'd pulled up. She swallowed hard and prayed her voice would come as strong and angry as she needed.

She pushed the photos across the desk. "One of these guys?"

He looked at the pages she handed him, and she hid her wince behind a deep breath and thought of her happy place.

"I could ask but the answer's going to take a while. I'll have to go back to Belize and talk to the locals he talked to." He shrugged and tossed the pages back on her desk, but he tilted his head, and his face pinched. "You okay?"

She nodded and swallowed against the very persistent ache in her belly.

His eyes went wide. "Should I get Grier?"

"No, tell me the rest." She put her hand over her stomach, waiting for the pain to pass.

"Fiona."

She smacked her hand on the desk. "Goddammit, Kye."

"Fine. They wanted to know if he's been there, if he has a place, if there's anyone he's close to." He stood and walked around to stand beside her. "Fiona, when's your baby due?"

"In a couple of weeks." The pain subsided, and she shoved his hand away. "How long ago were they there?"

"Last week."

Fuck. She waved him away. "Stop hovering over me and get back in your chair."

He laughed and walked around her desk to his seat. "Eli was grumpy during labor, too."

Grumpy? She wasn't grumpy. She was her normal sunshiny self. And if she was even a little grumpy, it was a hundred percent his fault and had nothing to do with...

"Shit!" Another sharp stab, and this one stole her breath.

He rocketed to his feet. "I'm getting Grier."

"Kye, I will kill you if you open that door." She inhaled a couple of short breaths. "Please. Tell me the rest." He didn't open the door, but neither did he turn toward her. She pulled her gun from the drawer, and he turned at the sound of the metal slide pulling a shell into the chamber.

"You're gonna shoot me."

"Dreamed of it since you took him away, and I'm not in a very stable mood right now. Tell. Me. The. Rest." She kept the gun pointed at him even as she bent to try to ease the pain in her back.

"I don't know, Fiona. I know he's in danger. They made threats and I got on a plane. I've been waiting for him to leave all day and he didn't so..." He pleaded with his eyes. "Fiona... come on. Let me get Grier."

She dropped her pistol-holding hand to the desk and held on to the edge with a white-knuckled grip. "Yeah."

A second later, Grier'd swept her into his arms

against his chest and carried her through the club to deposit her into the passenger seat of her car.

He took a couple of sideways glances at her as Kye climbed in the backseat and the rest of the guys followed on their bikes. It was a parade of Screaming Demons behind her car and damned if she cared. When she realized she was still holding it, she handed Grier her gun.

He smiled, but she saw the fear in his eyes, fear mirrored in her gut. "Good. I was afraid you might shoot me."

"Probably why you should keep it. Because if this gets worse, I might." She ended with a smile, and Kye laughed.

"She's probably not kidding. Eli wanted me dead by the time the baby came."

Of all the people to be sharing this ride, how had Kye ended up in her car? "Why's he here?"

Kye dropped a hand on her shoulder. "Moral support."

"I don't need your moral anything." She bit the words from behind clenched teeth. No way did she want him there, and as she was about to threaten him with Hamilton if he didn't jump out the back door, the world dimmed to black.

* * *

THREE HOURS. And Grier had counted every tick of the clock since they'd whisked Fiona into surgery, since he'd been banished, along with every other Demon and Kye to the waiting room.

"Fuck. What's taking so long?"

"Mass Gen is a good hospital. And they're taking care of her, Grier." Kye squeezed his shoulder, apparently unworried about the scowls coming his way from almost everyone in the room.

"They better be," Hamilton muttered.

He waited another hour before a doctor, not Fiona's doctor, came out. "Mr. Owen?" Grier stood and a line of friends dropped in behind him. "Your daughter is healthy and strong. They're getting her cleaned up and ready right now. Your wife suffered some complications, but she's in recovery, and we'll take you to her as soon as she's awake."

"What happened? She was fine this morning." He didn't miss the glare Hamilton shot Kye, but he tried to concentrate on the complicated medical jargon spewing forth from the doctor until his need to see Fiona took over. "Can I please see my wife? I just... I need to see her."

And goddammit, he didn't want to break down here, not in front of all these guys.

The doctor nodded. "I'll have a nurse come and get

you. But just you for today, okay? She can have other visitors when she's… better."

"Okay." He didn't give a damn if anyone else got to see her. But he couldn't very well leave Kye sitting in a waiting room with twenty motorcycle thugs who wanted him dead. He glanced at Hamilton. "Don't kill him. And don't let him get killed. Fiona might still want to talk to him."

Hamilton respecting authority, even Grier's authority, was a sight to behold. The single nod, the placid expression. "Want me to watch him?"

"Just take him to my house. You can wait with him if you want. Just leave him in one piece until I get there."

Worry etched Hamilton's face. "Let me know how Fiona's doing, okay?" He looked down at his shoes. "And the kid."

Grier squeezed the big guy's biceps. "Yeah. I will." He turned to Kye. "Ham is going to take you back to my place." His place with Fiona was more her place than his, but he loved it there. The little touches she put on everything. Hell, he even loved the lacy curtains she had hanging in the bedroom and the soaps shaped like pointy little hummingbirds that were *not* to be used, the guest towels that were *only for guests* and not him…

"Is he going to kill me?" The only indication Kye was serious was a little flicker of worry in his eyes.

"Might rough you up a little. You're scrappy. You can

handle him." Grier tried to joke, forced a smile, then turned to hide his tears.

He followed the nurse down a hallway, through a set of double doors, into another hallway and finally to a room at the end. He stood outside the door, took a deep breath to prepare for whatever awaited him behind the door, then walked in.

Fiona, so lively, so larger than life, looked small and frail with the white blanket tucked around her and the bed so much bigger than her small frame. Her red hair made flames on the pillow. Her left foot poked out of the blanket at the opposite edge of the bed.

She didn't stir, even when the legs of the chair ground against the white tiled floor when he pulled it closer to the bed. When he sat, he took her hand and held it through the rail. Warm. Small. He kissed the knuckles and gave a squeeze, then brought it to rest against his cheek as tears leaked out of his eyes.

"Hey." Her voice, small and quiet, brought him to his feet. "What's wrong? Did I die?"

He laughed. "No. Thank God."

"Good. Because I did not want to have to tell God he needed a new decorator." She smiled. "Have you seen her yet?"

"No. I came to see you. They were doing something with her. I don't know." All he cared about was Fiona, was letting her know he never wanted to lose her. His throat tightened with emotion and tears he couldn't seem to control today filled his eyes. The last thing he wanted was to blubber like some damned baby. He sniffed and shook his head. "You look good."

He'd seen her made up for a night out. He'd seen her in clothes that cost more than his bike. But never before had she been as beautiful as she was now.

She chuckled and laid a hand low on her stomach. "Oh, such a sweet lie."

"It's true. You are beautiful."

"You're just saying that because I had your baby today."

He grinned. "Yes, you did. That probably entitles you to some kind of present. Something big and shiny." Diamonds, maybe. But then he considered how much money he didn't have. Hell, he might just as well promise her the moon. He couldn't buy it any more than he could afford a diamond.

"I would rather just have you." She tugged him closer with the hand still attached to hers.

Grier leaned over the rail and kissed her lightly. Best kiss of his life. "I love you, Fiona."

Not that he hadn't thought it or said it before, but this time, he felt it all the way to his toes. Grier Owen loved Fiona Strong-Owen. And it was going to take a wrecking ball or a SWAT team escort to make him leave her again.

13

Fiona waited until Grier went to the cafeteria before she tried feeding the baby. And failed. Her daughter wouldn't latch. She would only cry. Her still nameless baby didn't want to eat from her mother, didn't want to be held by her either if the crying and squirming meant anything.

She looked down at her poor starving baby and tears filled her eyes. What was she doing? She didn't know how to be a mother, had no idea how to even feed her baby. What happened when she needed to be changed? Or bathed? Or told about boys? Or sex? Oh, God. Fiona wasn't ready to be a mother.

Her shoulders shook and she sobbed as the baby continued kicking and waving her tiny fist at Fiona's exposed breast. Fiona tried again, offered her nipple only to have the baby shake her head. "Oh, God. Why won't you eat for me?"

She pushed the button for the nurse and waited while the baby continued to squall. This couldn't be the way her next eighteen years were going to go. But as she had the thought, she knew. This would be exactly how it went. Mother and daughter butting heads over things as simple as food and as complex as life and what it all meant. Of course they would battle. And Fiona would have to be strong, would have to be the one who set the rules and the pace.

She swallowed her fear and her tears and repositioned the baby then offered her nipple again. And this time she waited… waited… and finally, the baby latched and Fiona breathed out softly. "There we go."

She smoothed the baby's hair forward, smiled as if she'd achieved world peace and solved global warming, then marveled at her baby. Grier's nose, Fiona's hair, Grier's eyes, Fiona's mouth and chin. Damn. She'd wanted the baby to have Grier's chin. Still beautiful. The most beautiful little person she'd ever seen.

This time her eyes filled with happy tears, brimming with love and happiness. "Your mommy is a big crybaby." Her daughter didn't seem to care and Fiona cradled her closer.

Grier stood in the doorway, his cheeks wet, his eyes

leaking. "This keeps up, we're going to have to buy stock in a tissue company."

Fiona nodded. "I have hormones to blame. What's your problem?"

She watched him walk into the room, taller than she'd ever seen him.

He stood over the bed and brushed his finger down the baby's cheek. "I just love my family."

And he'd never really had one, not one that was all his, but if she spent too much time thinking about that, she wouldn't be able to stop crying. She nodded. "Me, too."

"So what are we going to name this little beauty?" His voice was thick as he stood over them, his finger still caressing the baby's cheek.

She'd had so many names picked out, but none of them seemed to be right. None of them captured the beauty that was her daughter. "What do you think?"

He tilted his head. "Well. I kind of promised Max…"

"No." She watched the baby's eyelids flutter against her cheeks even as her mouth continued working. This would be a strong little girl who deserved a strong name. But also something as beautiful as she was. "Maybe we should think on it. Try some things out."

Grier nodded. "Do you have any favorites?" When she shook her head, he pulled out his phone and typed into the screen. "Okay... here we go." He scrolled. "Harper? Ivy? Paris…" His head bobbed from one side to the other. "Piper? Teagen, Tenley, Willow…" He rattled off a few more.

"You have to tell me what they mean. Her name should mean something." Not that she had any idea what her own name meant.

"Okay." He continued scrolling. "Zoey means 'light' or 'life.' Aurora means 'dawn.' Caroline means 'small and strong.'" He paused. "Jocelyn means 'joyous.'"

"What about Hope?" It seemed appropriate since this baby had given Fiona a new optimism for the future.

Grier put his phone on the bed and looked at their daughter, such love shining in his eyes, Fiona could've probably suggested anything and he would have agreed. "I like it."

Fiona nodded. "Do you really like it or are you just saying that because you think I'll burst into tears if you say you don't like it?" He smiled and she knew the latter was true. "Hey, *Kermit*, our baby is going to have this name for the rest of her life."

"Whoa. Pulling out the real name…" He clicked his tongue against his teeth. "All right, woman. I like the name Hope. I also liked London, Paris, and Brooklyn. Just because they're cute names. I also don't think we should stick her with a big name full of meaning that she has to live up to. It's a lot of pressure to put on a newborn." He ended strong and Fiona smiled. "What?"

"You're right."

And at four p.m., after hours of fussing, three feedings and a few hundred kisses and photos, Grier and Fiona pulled the baby's name from one of her tiny little hats—London Hope Owen.

FIONA WATCHED Grier sleep on the sofa with the baby on his chest. Oh, God. If he turned over, the baby would either topple to the floor or be trapped between him and the back of the couch. But they looked so peaceful and comfortable... her adorable family. In the three weeks since they'd brought the baby home, he'd woken with her every night for feedings, changed more than his fair share of diapers, and taken over all the household and club related chores.

And now he'd fallen asleep holding their baby. Fiona's heart fluttered.

"Hey." Grier opened his eyes and smiled. "Every time I wake up, I keep hoping this isn't all a dream."

"And every time I wake up, I know it has to be." Oh, God. Where had all this sappiness come from? She was Fiona Strong. *Strong.* Not some big bawling baby who looked at her husband and their child and wept. Fiona

Strong didn't weep. Except she did. More often than even Grier knew. She cried in the morning when she woke next to him. Cried when she looked at how perfect her baby had turned out. Cried when she changed a diaper, or fed the baby, or when Grier made her plate at dinner or ran her bathwater, or any of the thousand things he did for her. Every single one reduced her to a crying slop of woman.

And it had to stop.

She forced the tears back with a quick graze of her fingers over her eyes, a deep swallow and a calm, centering breath. "Are you just sitting here watching me sleep?" He grinned. "If it wasn't so damned sexy it would be a little creepy."

She rolled her eyes. "If you must know, I was thinking about cooking some supper."

"Really?"

No. She'd been staring. "Yes. Well, ordering supper anyway. I might dial it myself tonight."

He unfolded his body, sat up and in one swift motion, situated the baby on his right arm. "I could take you out. Jez is dying for some one-on-one time with London."

Leave her baby? Even with Jez, Fiona just wasn't ready. Besides, the best memories she had were of the last weeks, at home, alone, with Grier and the baby. "Let's stay in."

"We could go to the club. Guys haven't seen you in a while. Then the baby can go."

She hadn't been there since the day she went into labor. Neither did she have any desire to go. "No. I just want to have a quiet night. Just the three of us." For that matter, the baby could go anywhere they went. That was the purpose of the car seat and diaper bag and stroller, the baby paraphernalia currently collecting dust in the nursery.

"Okay." But he frowned. "Are you afraid to take her out anywhere?"

Of course she was. There were germs and people and what if someone bumped into the baby and elbowed her or... and this one scared her most... what if she let someone hold the baby and they dropped her? No. Home was better. Fiona could protect London inside these four walls.

"Of course not. I just don't feel like going tonight."

Grier nodded. "Okay. You order dinner. I'll change the baby and we'll meet back here in five minutes." His soft smile made her feel like a phony, like a fraud, but since he didn't mention her lie, she didn't either. And that, as of late, summed up their relationship.

GRIER SAT in Fiona's frilly office and missed all of Max's hardwood accents, the copper and gold accents, the beer tap he'd kept in the corner where the bar had been. And since he'd sent Kye back to Belize, he missed having someone to talk to. He was in charge until Fiona got back to work and he couldn't risk looking weak in front of any of the guys.

Hamilton sat across from him. They'd already taken care of all the business. Why Hamilton hadn't left yet must have meant something. Fiona had probably told him, but he didn't remember and Hamilton was a man of few words, so asking probably wouldn't get him anywhere.

"Was there something else?" Well, he couldn't just sit there and let Hamilton stare.

"We have a pretty reliable lead on Sedotal and Carr."

They'd been in this room for more than an hour and this should have been the lead story of the day. "Yeah?" But no point looking over-anxious.

"Funeral home." He pulled out the picture of Max with Hamilton, One-eye and Carr. He pointed to the fifth man in the picture, a guy Grier now knew as O'Shea—nothing else, just O'Shea. "Killed last week. Rammed his bike into the back end of a minivan."

"And?"

"Word on the street is Carr was still tight with O'Shea. Smart money says he'll be there."

Grier nodded. "Then so will we." He wanted these fuckers bad. Bad enough he'd stake the place out himself. Give up time with Fiona and London to be the one watching the place. "So we wait until they leave, then we follow. And we keep a man on them."

"Probably won't be that easy."

Of course it wouldn't. It would take all of them working together. A solid plan. Something foolproof. This was his chance to make up for his every failing to Fiona. One chance to get this right.

* * *

SAGE NODDED TO THE DOOR. "There he is."

Carr. But Grier wanted Sedotal. He wanted to kill him. Slowly. Painfully. One fucking limb at a time for what Sedotal had done to Fiona. Hamilton waited until Carr drove a block down before he pulled the rental car onto the road. He would follow Carr while the rest of the club waited for Sedotal to come out. They had all the exits covered. No way would he get out without being seen.

Men and women exited the funeral home. The sun faded. The last car left the lot and still, no sign of Sedotal. Had he somehow slipped past them? A gnawing in Grier's gut said no, but when the funeral director came out and locked the deadbolt, there was no denying it.

Sedotal had escaped. They'd damned sure seen him go in.

He smacked the butt of his hand on the top curve of the steering wheel in Max's Mercedes, the only car of her father's Fiona hadn't sold. She'd be pissed if she knew he'd taken his frustration out on the car, but damn it, they'd lost the one man he'd been counting on ending tonight. At least he had Hamilton on Carr. Maybe the father would lead them to the son. Grier had to hope so.

He glanced at Sage whose eyes remained pointed at the door of the funeral home. This was supposed to be easy. They'd planned everything. And now he was sitting in a car, holding his dick, yet again, and Sedotal was out there somewhere, waiting and laughing.

"Where the hell did he go?"

Sage glanced at him. "I don't know."

"Check with Jim. Maybe he went out the back." Grier waited while Sage talked with Jim. And from Sage's voice, the news wasn't good. When Sage hung up, Grier stared at him. "What?"

"If he came out, he didn't come out the back."

Fuck. Grier started the car. The place was empty, dark, and quiet. No point in sitting here anymore.

He needed to get back to the club, find out where they'd gone wrong, and pray like hell Hamilton didn't lose Carr. So long as they had Carr, they could at least track him and maybe use him to their benefit.

He drove back to the clubhouse and Hamilton called Sage to give them an address. "Tell him to sit on it and watch for Sedotal. I'll send back-up."

God. This had to work. Now, he wasn't just letting Fiona down, but his daughter. And that had to stop.

iona hadn't had a shower in two days. Her hair hung in scraggly mats against her head and her shirt would forever be stained by the amount of spit on her shoulder. She'd been doing this alone for the last three days. Grier had been out watching a house. Talking to other adults. Breathing air that wasn't tainted by the smell of diapers and dirty laundry. But every time Fiona made a move to do anything that resembled cleaning herself or the house, London cried as if she'd stubbed her toe, which Fiona did, her own anyway, twice.

As she walked the floor, bouncing the baby in one arm, the door opened and closed. Grier walked in. His hair hadn't fared much better than hers, which wasn't much consolation. "Hey."

On one hand, she hadn't seen anyone she'd missed

more. Max could have walked in and she wouldn't have been so happy to see him. On the other hand, Grier had left her alone for what had come to feel like months rather than days. She glared at him when all she really wanted to do was to rush into his arms and let him hold her.

"What?" He hung his head. "Fiona, I'm tired. I don't feel like doing this with you right now."

"What about her? Feel like explaining to her where you've been? You haven't even looked at your daughter." And if she was fair, which she didn't feel at all like being, she would have given him more than a three-second chance.

He walked past her to the kitchen. He poured a glass of water, spilled a few drops on the floor, and turned as Fiona threw a dishtowel at him then stalked across the floor to grab it before he could and clean up the tiny mess. "Let me get that for you." The acid in her voice should have melted him into a puddle, but Grier stiffened.

When he turned, she was close enough to see every red streak—and there were hundreds—in the whites of his eyes, every line of fatigue on his face. The smile when he slipped an arm around her waist and pulled her in with the baby between them. "You're beautiful. And I've missed you."

She rested her head on his shoulder. "I missed you, too."

The kiss on her forehead was a bonus. "Let's put this little lady in bed and run a bath. I'll wash your back if you wash mine."

Oh, that all sounded so heavenly. And tiring. "Side offer?" He grinned. "Baby to bed, *shower*, and snuggles in bed?" A bath would just eat up so much time.

"You bet." He gave her a squeeze, took the baby and smiled down at her. Fiona wanted to capture this moment forever, hang onto it, because something inside of her, deep in her guts, told her things were changing and there was nothing she could do to stop it.

* * *

AN HOUR LATER, she cuddled next to him, her head on his chest, her leg thrown over his. Something about this man had always made her feel... everything. When she was a teenager, he'd made her heart flutter. When she'd come home from college for visits, he'd made her entire body flutter. And now...

She pressed a kiss over his heart. "Do you ever want to just... get out of here? Go somewhere just... away? The three of us."

He sat up. "Sometimes, but this is your inheritance,

Fiona. Could you really walk away from it?" Something in his eyes told her he wanted her to say yes.

She shrugged. "I don't know. But sometimes, I just want us to be… not involved in this whole world. Guns and drugs and car parts…"

"Where would you want to go?"

Oh, that question. Over the last two days, she'd imagined a hundred places, a hundred houses with white picket fences, a minivan, London in soccer shorts or a tutu or a princess dress with fairy wings and a wand whirling circles on the lawn, unaware and unafraid that some rival biker gang would want to snatch her up as a bargaining tool… or worse.

"Mayberry." Where the only thing she had to worry about was Barney giving her a ticket for parking in front of a hydrant. She could get a job that let her be home with the baby. Maybe she'd even buy one of those cooking aprons and learn how to fry chicken and steam vegetables.

"Wouldn't you miss all of this?"

Because she couldn't be sure if he meant him or the club or even the weather, she leaned over him for a kiss. "As long as I have you and London, nothing else matters." When she moved to pull away, he held onto her and pressed his lips against hers again in a kiss so slow and sweet, she ached for more. But he released her. And she settled into his side. "Someday."

It was a nice dream anyway.

One that held her over until the baby woke an hour or so later demanding food and to be changed. "I'll get her."

Grier pushed back the blankets and climbed out of bed. When he returned, London in his arms, he smiled down at the baby as he handed her to Fiona. "You changed her?"

"Yeah." He slid between the sheets and sat up, letting the baby hold his finger, and for being such a little thing, nothing in her life had ever made Fiona's heart fuller. "She looks like you, babe."

"And you."

He grinned. "I don't think I'm overstating anything when I say I have one beautiful family. The *most* beautiful family."

Instead of replying she took it all in. Her husband. Her baby. Her life. What more could she have asked for?

She looked up at Grier. Not asking about the club had kept her sane. A new baby, the ever-changing body, the unexpected demands of motherhood all gave her enough to worry about without adding rival clubs, added security and a man-hunt on top of it all. But now, in the darkness, with Grier by her side, she needed to know. "How are things?"

"We have Carr under surveillance. No sign of Sedotal." He spoke in a cute little baby voice as he shook

London's hand with his finger. "He could teach a class in going off the grid."

"Do you know anything?"

"Not much. Carr is over in Manchester with his woman. Takes her out for coffee in the morning, a little mayhem before lunch, then returns in the afternoon."

Fiona nodded. Maybe they were going about this wrong. "Every day?" Grier shifted to look at her. "I was just thinking… maybe instead of him, someone should talk to her. See if his pillow talk is as interesting as I would bet it is."

The thing about guys like Willy Carr was that they loved to brag about their accomplishments. And who better to tell than the woman he was banging? Maybe they could use the woman to find out if he had any aspirations that would affect the club. And if she knew where to find Sedotal, that would be a bonus.

"I could send Jez."

"Maybe." But everyone knew Jez. Knew she was a Demon Hell Kat. And if Carr had been friends with her father for any length of time, chances were, he already knew her and it would be risky to send Jez in to make friends with the woman. "Or you could send…" Had it not been her best option, she would have rather slit her own throat than say the name. "Autumn." Jez apparently trusted Grier's former girlfriend enough to take her off the wall and that was enough for Fiona. And she would push her jealousy aside long enough to use Autumn for what the club needed. Besides, if Autumn screwed them over, Fiona would end her. And that would be that.

* * *

GRIER AND SAGE sat across the street from the three-story house in Manchester. The kind of house he wanted to give Fiona. With a place like this, whoever owned it could have made a fortune by splitting the house into apartments, but it looked like a single-family had taken residence. There were bikes in the yard of all sizes, apparently for kids of all ages. A car wedged between this house and the one next to it. A chain-link fence surrounding the front yard. The gate wiggled in the breeze and the clanking of the metal kept Grier focused, more alert than he ever remembered being.

They hadn't wired Autumn, and now he wished they had. Not only because he didn't trust her—their relationship had been born of nothing more than sex, so he didn't know her well enough to know whether or not he could—but because she was in there, and if Sedotal had managed to get past them out of the funeral home, he certainly could here, and he would recognize Autumn from his time at the club.

He didn't breathe freely until she walked out the gate

and onto the sidewalk. She climbed in the backseat and pulled the door shut behind her. "Well?"

Sage twisted in the seat as Grier took off toward home.

Autumn chuckled. "She's nice."

Grier rolled his eyes at her in the mirror. "Didn't send you in there to make a new best friend, Autumn. What did she say?"

"She said Carr has never been around so much, and now she's pregnant. He's big on family."

What the hell did Grier care whether or not he liked Sedotal or hated him? He sighed. This wasn't the intel he wanted.

"Apparently he has kids all over creation. The only one she knows is Tyler. Said she'd set me up if I want." Autumn giggled. "Anyway, Carr has a cabin, somewhere South. On the ocean." She pulled a picture from somewhere behind her. "I don't know if this will help, but I took it. It's the cabin. Looks like Florida, maybe California. See the palm trees? Tyler is probably holed up there waiting for… whatever to happen before he reappears."

For *whatever* to happen? Goddammit. She was supposed to find out exactly what *whatever* meant. Sounded more like she'd enjoyed a leisurely tea while he suffered in the car listening to Sage sing along with the radio. "Anything else?"

"He might actually be waiting for permission before

he comes back. Seems Daddy and his boy had a falling out. She didn't know exactly about what, but she knew it was bad. It was bad enough that Carr sent Tyler away and told him not to come back until he had his head out of his ass. Something about one of Carr's other kids. That was all she knew." Autumn spoke as if she was a newscaster reading the day's big headlines. "Anyway, there's a man-sized hole in the wall where he threw Tyler through it. Must have been a big fight."

Other kids? They didn't have one damned piece of intel about other kids. Despite that, Autumn had done what he'd asked. She'd found out where to find Tyler Sedotal. Before Grier could tell her, Sage jumped in. "You did great, Autumn." He shot her a smile over the seat. His pick-up smile. And if Sage wanted her, that was up to them.

"Thanks." And she reached forward to tousle Sage's hair.

He grinned over his shoulder at her and Grier drove faster. He missed his wife and his baby, and he finally had something important to tell her. But first, he wanted to get back to the club and make a few calls. He needed to find out about these other kids of Carr's.

Fiona stared up at him. It had been three weeks since she'd talked about leaving Pine Hill for Mayberry, but when Grier walked in the door, she had her laptop on her lap and the baby attached to her breast.

He leaned over the back of the sofa, and she pointed to a brick ranch house on the screen. "It's a little south of Chicago."

"And a big hello to you, too." But he took the laptop and scrolled through the pictures before he handed it back then kissed the spot under her ear that made her motor run. "You should check Belize. Sun and sand. Life's slower there. Mayberry with palm trees." And he missed it. Especially with the cold weather blowing in colder every night. He hadn't ridden his bike in days and picturing Fiona in a bikini didn't hurt the fantasy of living with her there either.

Fiona tilted her chin, exposing more of her neck for his lips. "I burned supper."

"Not hungry." He murmured the words against her skin. "For food." Not only did he miss his bike, but he missed his wife.

"That's too bad. Jez is in the kitchen making meatloaf and potatoes." Every sound she breathed made his dick throb with more urgency. And then the words hit their mark.

Damn. Jez was one room away and his dick was hard enough to burst through his jeans. He straightened and adjusted, then semi-limped to the bedroom. Fiona followed. She shut the door behind her and pushed Grier against the wall then angled her body so his thigh ended up between her legs and her hands were free to go after his belt.

"Just because I can't yet…" She flicked his jeans open and stroked her hand along his cock. "Doesn't mean you can't."

Grier pushed his head back and closed his eyes as she knelt in front of him and tugged his jeans down. "Fiona." He wanted to be a big enough man to tell her he would wait for her, that this wasn't necessary, but… she wrapped her mouth around him and sucked him deep into her mouth, and he couldn't think of another word to say.

She worked him, head bobbing and hand squeezing in perfect unison until he moaned, threw his head back and tangled his fingers in her hair. The things she did with her tongue made his balls tighten. Oh, God.

"Fiona. I'm gonna…" And he exploded in her mouth.

She continued sucking until she had taken every last drop. Then she stood, winked, and smiled. "How's that hello?"

He nodded and when the brain fog lifted, he pulled his jeans up. "I think that's the one we should go with every day."

"You think so?"

This was the woman of his dreams. And that she was his until death did they part still amazed him. He pulled her in for a hug. "How long until you can…?" He nodded toward the bed and wiggled his eyebrows.

"Not much longer."

It had already been a month. Hard to believe his daughter was a month old. And the knowledge made him smile. "Can't be soon enough." He wanted to hold her. Touch her. Bring her to the brink and pull her back until she begged him for release.

"You're telling me."

He stared long enough that she squirmed out of his arms, and he missed her. "Come back." He reached for her and she side-stepped so he came back with an armful of air.

"I left the baby with Jez who is already making our dinner and cleaned the house while I napped with the baby." She smiled. "I just wanted to see you with that look on your face."

"What look?" The curse of Grier Owen was that he couldn't hide much of what he was feeling unless he concentrated. And with his dick in Fiona's mouth, he could concentrate on nothing else.

"The   I-love-my-wife-I-love-my-life-and-please-don't-stop-sucking-me-off-look." She had such a smug smile, and he loved it. He loved everything about her.

"This look?" He threw his head back and opened his

mouth much the same as he had a moment ago. "Or this one?" He crossed his eyes and panted.

"That's the one."

Since the baby had come, they hadn't had much time to enjoy each other. He missed that, too. Definitely something they would have to work on.

15

Never in Fiona's life had she found a man more enticing, especially while he was doing something as mundane as mowing the lawn. But that sheen of sweat, that swagger to his walk, the way his muscles extended and contracted as he pushed and pulled the mower across the backyard was hot.

She fanned herself with her hand. When that did nothing to cool her off, she sopped her forehead with a towel. There was something to be said for seventy-degree, bright sunshiny days in December. Something else to be said for having ignored yard maintenance until now, and even more to say about the way her husband looked, bare-chested, in basketball shorts.

The baby cooed in her swing watching some cartoon show while Fiona stood at the backdoor gawking at Grier, knowing she'd promised to decorate the tree while he worked outside, but unable to move. Grier had a thousand looks she loved, but domesticated was one of her favorites.

When the mower died, she waited until he walked up the steps and opened the door before she moved. "You're hot." And she wasn't talking temperature-wise.

"And sweaty." He wrinkled his nose and walked around her to the cabinet for a glass he filled with ice and water. Fiona couldn't stop staring. Nor did she want to. He smiled. "What?"

She kicked off her shoes and smiled as she ran her finger down his chest. "I got cleared by the doctor." And just in the nick of time, too. She'd had enough of waiting, enough of getting Grier off while she suffered without.

"Yeah?"

"Oh yeah. Fit as a fiddle and… ready." She unbuttoned the first three buttons of her shirt before he reached to stop her.

"Can we get a sitter for tonight?"

Tonight? He was planning to make her wait? After she'd rushed home from the doctor to find him mowing, worked herself into a frenzy watching, and was now about to burst with wanting him?

"Probably, but…" Dammit. She didn't need some grand gesture. She needed his dick. Needed an earthshattering orgasm. Needed Grier to take off his pants and make some serious moaning happen.

"Good. I'm going to shower and get ready." He walked past her again.

She put a hand on his chest. "I could help you prime the pump."

"Nice play on words. But no. My pump's been primed for a while." He kissed her softly, but quickly. A tease and not nearly enough. "Tonight. I promise."

She'd stopped on the way home for condoms she'd left on the bed. They were still there when Jez came to pick up the baby and Fiona hid her new lingerie under her new dress. She picked a pair of fuck-me pumps in a deep shade of blue that matched the dress and walked out into the living room where Grier waited in a pair of jeans and a button-down.

Her heart thumped hard and her breath came in short puffs. They'd be lucky to make it to whatever restaurant he insisted on dragging her to. "Okay, I'm ready."

He turned and his eyes blazed a path up her body. "Yes, you are." The look was raw and hot and Fiona's panties went damp.

"Shall we go?" She didn't add, 'and get this over with', but her tone said it for her. She didn't need any damned food. She needed Grier naked and on top of her. Or under her. Or behind her. She didn't care which.

He nodded slowly. "I made reservations at…"

She didn't care. Not when he helped her with her coat—the temperature had dropped by thirty degrees in the last few hours with a cold front—or when he guided her toward the Mercedes.

As he drove, he slid his hand across her thigh, under the hem of her skirt, then inched toward the white-hot heat of her pussy. She slid down in the seat urging him closer, moaning when he brushed his finger over her clit then drew away. "You're so wet." His voice, husky and deep, washed over her.

She slipped off her seatbelt and leaned across the console. Grier wasn't the only one who could tease. "That's because I've been thinking about your cock all day long." She ran her tongue over the shell of his ear. "Let's find a nice secluded spot. You can move the seat back and I'll—"

She didn't finish because the car jerked when Grier braked hard. Their bumper tapped the car in front of them.

"Fuck." He'd thrown an arm in front of her to keep her from lurching forward, but he dropped it now. "Are you okay?"

She was fine. Less horny now, but fine. "Yeah. You?"

"Well, officer, I closed my eyes thinking about fucking my wife, and when I opened them, the car in front of me was stopped." He chuckled. "Maybe I'll get a judge with a hot wife who understands how it is."

"Or maybe we can just turn it in to the insurance and be on our way?" This was not the best way to start date night.

Fiona waited while Grier exchanged insurance information with the other driver, then for him to give a short statement to the police, then for the tow truck to arrive to haul away Max's car. It wasn't until they were in a taxi that she got to touch him again. She laid his hand in her lap and tugged the hem of her skirt up.

He pulled her panties to the side and whispered, "Don't make a sound." His finger slipped along her clit and she breathed in slow until he pushed it inside her. He stared ahead as if watching the road, not looking at her, but his half-smile said he knew exactly what he was doing.

His finger dipped in and out as he used his thumb to circle her clit, and she tried not to pant, tried not to moan, even when they pulled in front of the restaurant and he withdrew. Before he opened the door to get out, he kissed her cheek and whispered, "You can finish inside."

Oh, God. She'd be lucky to make it that long. He guided her through the rotating door. A crystal chandelier hung overhead in the foyer and the carpet was a deep burgundy that matched the shade of wallpaper crossed with gold. This was opulent. Expensive. A gorgeous place. And she didn't give a damn about any of it. She wanted to find the nearest bathroom, drag her husband in behind her, and fuck him until the walls shook and the big fancy chandelier danced on its chain.

But she waited, standing beside him as he gave the maitre d' his name and another man came to lead them to their round booth. He slid in next to her. This was secluded. Had she not passed them on the way to theirs, she wouldn't have known there was another table in the entire place.

When the man walked away, Grier smiled and leaned in to kiss her. His tongue played at the seam of her lips, and he drew her hand beneath the table, used his to guide it up her thigh, so near her pussy, but he pulled them both back. "Not yet."

She groaned, soft but from low in her belly. She needed Grier. Now. She pushed his hand away. "You're such a tease."

He tossed his napkin on the table. "I'll crawl under this table right now and make you scream loud enough we both get thrown out of here and probably arrested." Worth it in her book, but he continued before she could tell him. "Or… we can make this night last until we get upstairs and you can see what I have planned for you."

"But you said I could finish once we got inside."

"And you will. Just… not. Yet."

She grinned at the promise behind his words. "Fine."

* * *

GRIER WAS one sultry look from an explosion in his pants. He hadn't been kidding about crawling under the table. If she'd asked, he would've, and now as his punishment for not, he had to watch her practically making love with her mouth to a spoon full of chocolate mousse. What this woman could do with eating utensils should've been illegal.

He signaled for the check and paid then on legs made of jelly, helped Fiona from the booth. "You are killing me, woman." She had an extra sway to her hips, and if that dress dipped any lower...

With the room key burning a hole in his pocket, they walked to the elevator, not touching, but the electricity sparking between them reminded him of how he'd felt the first time with her. How badly he'd wanted her, needed to touch her. So much so, he had almost embarrassed himself. But not tonight.

Tonight, he had plans for her.

In the elevator, too crowded for much more than a few illicit brushes of her hand against his zipper, he tried to hold his shit together and not give the rest of the folks sharing the lift a porn show. But when she reached low to full-on rub his cock, he groaned and the woman in front of him turned to glare.

Fiona smiled. "The steak didn't agree with him."

The woman jerked around and inched forward away from them. How the hell was this damned thing so crowded on a Tuesday night in December?

Fiona continued to toy with him—a debt he'd be more than happy to repay once they were alone—as the car stopped on various floors letting passengers out until they were alone. He pressed her against the mirrored wall, used his knee to spread her legs, then fit himself between.

She moaned as he ground his hips once into hers. "I should bend you over my knee right here for teasing me like that." He growled the words against her ear and was rewarded with a whimper. He squeezed her ass then gave it a little tap. This time she squealed and melded her mouth to his. His cock strained against his jeans and thank God, the doors whooshed open. Their stop.

She slipped off the shoes, shoes she would be putting back on, and jogged beside him down the hall. He'd been one second from lowering that exposed zipper running from her shoulder blade to her ass. At the door to their room, he pulled the tab with one hand and slipped the keycard into the slot with the other. She walked inside and let the dress fall off to pool around her feet. And

Grier's tongue rolled up. He'd be lucky not to swallow the damned thing.

Her lingerie, black and barely there, was a one-piece with a thin line of lace that ran along her stomach with a thinner sliver tucked between her ass cheeks. He wanted to rip the damned thing off. With his teeth.

He pushed her back onto the bed and laid next to her, tracing a finger along the fabric that curved over the swell of her breasts. She had new curves, mouth-watering curves, and he wanted to take his time and explore every single one, but her hands clawed at his shirt and her mouth attacked his throat.

It seemed he spent all of their bedroom time telling himself to slow it down, but if he didn't, their night would be over before it started. And this was one place he didn't plan to disappoint his Fiona. He rolled away and stood. "Come here."

She knee-walked across the bed, and if he could've listened, he was sure he would have heard his dick begging.

"Undress me." And it would take an act of God not to come in his jeans, but she liked when he told her what to do and tonight was for her. And, okay, for him.

Instead of taking each button and slipping it through its slot, she grabbed the two sides and yanked. The tap of tiny plastic buttons against the furniture was just another of those sounds working against him. Along with her moans and whimpers, the swish of her knees against the blanket, the vibration in his own throat.

She looked up and ran her tongue over the end of her finger while she batted her eyes at him. "Oops. I ruined your shirt."

"It's okay."

She clicked her tongue against her teeth and shook her head. "I probably deserve a spanking."

When she turned to lay her head against the mattress, leaving her ass in the air, Grier shook his head. "You are a naughty girl."

"And you should spank me."

The way she said it as she rubbed her hand over her ass brought him closer to the edge. He brought his hand down, and she whimpered as she slid her finger into her pussy. "Do it again. Harder."

Oh, God. But he raised his hand and swatted her ass. "Turn over."

"No." She worked her finger over her clit and writhed against her hand. "Spank my ass."

Instead, he pulled her hand away. "You're not getting yourself off." He moved away from the bed to the chair where he'd stored a bag he'd dropped off earlier when Fiona was getting ready. Toys. A couple of those sexy as hell scarves. A bottle of warming massage oil.

He pulled out the massage oil. "Lay on your belly." Once he had her relaxed, then the real fun would begin.

He started with her feet, then her calves, kneading and pressing against muscle until she moaned in contentment. He moved up over her ass, soothing the light red handprint still visible, then trailed his hands in a slick line up her spine to her shoulders. He loved the feel of her skin, the twitch of her muscles as he smoothed and rubbed.

"Turn over."

Again, he started with her feet and moved his way up. He'd planned to go all the way to her shoulders again, but no way could he ignore the glistening wetness between her legs. He bent, intending only a quick kiss, but no way could he stop. Not when her breaths came in short desperate gasps, and she tasted like heaven. He pushed one of her knees up and held it there as he lapped and licked and sucked her clit into his mouth.

His cock ached, but he lifted his head and reached for the bag, pulled out a small vibrator he'd found just after he moved in. Switching it on, he ran it over her clit then slid it inside her. She shifted and he pushed it deeper then pulled it back as he lowered his head again. "You don't come until I'm inside you."

"Or you'll spank me again?"

"Or I'll close up shop and we go home." The hell. But she didn't have to know. He grinned against her clit and pushed the vibrator in and out twice before he sat up.

"Oh, God, Grier." She reached for him but he moved

away, still fucking her with her toy. The sounds she made excited every cell in his body.

"Have you ever watched yourself, Fiona?" That he could talk at all he considered one of his greatest accomplishments. "Let me video." He grunted the words and waited for her nod before he pulled out his phone and turned the camera on. "Touch yourself for me."

He scooted back and unfastened his zipper to relieve as much pressure as he dared, keeping the phone pointed toward her as she used one hand on the vibrator and the other on her clit.

"Don't come, Fiona." She slid the vibrator out and tossed it toward the chair then sat up to pull him down on top of her. The phone slid to the floor and he pushed his pants away as she wrapped her legs around his waist and attached her mouth to his.

He pumped into her, his cock so hard he was afraid he'd hurt her, but she met every thrust, every grind of his hips with her own.

"Grier!"

Her body twisted under his and her pussy tightened around him as he shot into her. It wasn't until he floated back to Earth that he realized. "Fiona, I forgot a condom."

She sighed and snuggled into his side. "I don't care. I'll have ten kids with you if you want."

He chuckled. "Definitely not ten." They only had the

one and barely managed to make time to see one another. Maybe in a few years they could try again. But from now until then, he'd happily use protection.

* * *

FIONA ONLY CALLED to check on the baby once, but she'd come four times. A victory for husband Grier even as Daddy Grier frowned.

Fiona hung up the phone. "She's fine."

"I assumed she would be." Not that he wouldn't have rushed to pick her up if Jez had any problems, but thank God, she hadn't. This was one night he really didn't want to end early. Fiona reclined and stretched languidly next to him. "I did some thinking about Mayberry." He'd thought about it a lot.

"A nice dream, huh?"

"Yeah." He gathered her close and planted a kiss against her scalp. "I could probably get a job fixing cars."

"Or you could be a stay at home dad, and I could work."

He smiled. Funny. "You mean drive the carpool and coach the soccer team?"

"Yeah." She nodded and rested her chin on her hands just over his heart. "You could bake cupcakes for the bake sales, join the PTA, be my love slave."

To be honest, when they'd first married, he'd thought

she would keep him away from the business rather than turn it all over to him. But he frowned at the wistfulness in her voice. "You missing work?"

She tilted her head from side to side. "I miss being out in the world."

Of course, she did. Being his wife wouldn't be enough for a woman like Fiona. He'd been stupid to ever let himself think it would. Of course, neither would Mayberry, but he didn't tell her. He could let her have this fantasy. "Come back to work."

"And leave the baby?" She shook her head. "No." In one long gulp, she downed the champagne from her flute. He'd ordered it shortly after round three ended and it arrived just before round four commenced. "Not with anybody but you. Or Jez and we can't ask her to give up her life to watch London."

"You could bring her along. Who's gonna tell you no?"

Only someone with a death wish.

"No." Fiona's refusal was as loud as it was adamant. "I want her to have a life free from danger and the illegal aspects of it all." She sat cross-legged in front of him. "I just want her to be able to choose."

He'd never realized how she felt about the club or having it pushed on her. Maybe that was why she'd surrendered control so easily. Or maybe it was the baby that had softened her outlook on things. Either way, part of him missed the old Fiona, the hard as a rock woman who spewed orders with the ferocity of a volcano and made sure the club's operations ran smoothly. Of course, the rest of him enjoyed this new, more easygoing woman wearing Fiona's body.

With all the new dangers facing them, Mayberry didn't sound so bad.

———

16

Fiona stared at Hamilton. He squirmed, too big for the small kitchen chair he sat in. A cup of coffee steamed in front of him. "Just thought you should know."

"Did you tell Grier?"

Hamilton looked down at the table, probably unsure of where his loyalties were supposed to lie since she'd all but surrendered control of everything to Grier. He shook his head and wrapped a meaty claw around his mug.

"How do you know, Hamilton? I mean… obviously there won't be any paperwork."

He sighed and even his sigh was big enough to ruffle the curtain next to him. "If I tell you, you can't fly off and do anything crazy. Because it wasn't just one person who kept this secret. It was all of them. Every single person involved. You dad, your mom, Jim." He looked down. "And Jez."

"And she just… what… told you?" When he nodded, Fiona's blood burst into flames in her veins. "Then you'd better tell me."

For a few minutes, he looked everywhere but at her. The floor. The ceiling. The countertop. "Jez was only fifteen when she met Will. Your dad was eighteen and Will was twenty-five. She was just a run-away who hitched a ride with a guy on a bike. I don't think she planned it. I don't think she knew what sleeping with Will would do." He stood and poured more coffee into his mug then turned to lean his back against the counter. His legs stretched out into the floor and he crossed the ankles before he looked up again. "But Will couldn't get enough. And she loved him. Right up until she turned up pregnant. Then that new car glow wore off and he started kicking her ass. I think maybe he hoped she would lose the kid. This was right when they were starting the club. Your dad and mom hadn't even met yet."

Apparently, these were important details and Fiona tried to focus, but this was a lot of information to digest without the aid of something eighty-proof. She went to the cabinet and pulled out a bottle of Grier's favorite whiskey. "Pour us a real drink. I think we need it."

She waited while he found glasses, held them under

the ice dispenser then poured them each four fingers before he came back to sit across from her. He took a long drink, drained more than half his glass, then sat back twisting it so the ice made a little clinking sound against the sides. "Anyway, your dad came in one night and Will had a gun to her head. Probably would've shot her, but your dad yanked him away. Will ended up with a gunshot wound, Jez went into labor, and when your dad came back to finish the job, he found the compound empty. Carr took all the money, the guns, the drugs, everything. Your dad and Jez and One-eye started over. Found this place. Only used the compound when the heat was too big. Your dad loved Jez, but she was too young. And then he met your mom and it was over between him and Jez until your mom died."

Funny, but he'd skipped over a lot. "Maybe you should tell me what happened to the baby."

Hamilton nodded and poured himself another glass. "All right." He sniffed and took another drink. "She kept the baby as long as she could, but Carr wouldn't leave her alone. He'd disappear for a while, run off doing God knows what then he'd be back, beating on her door, threatening her."

"Why didn't she leave?"

Fiona would have. She would've packed her shit and got the hell out of dodge before the kid had its first dirty diaper.

"She tried. And he tried to take the kid. Your dad saved her again. He beat Carr to within an inch of his life, but he just couldn't finish it."

"Bullshit. Max was never too weak to do a job, especially if he loved her as much as you say."

"Those boys grew up together. When your grandma died, Will's family took your dad in so he wouldn't have to go away from here." Hamilton sighed. "Anyway, after a while of hiding her, and Carr finding her… your dad made Jez give up the baby. He told her it was the only way to keep him safe. A few years later, Carr came back, they all made peace for a while—that's what everybody thought. That picture you had was from the last weekend they were all up at the compound together. Jez took it. That last night, he tried to kill her, tried to make her tell him where she'd taken the baby. By then, she couldn't. Even if she wanted to. She'd lost track of him. She tried to keep up. When you tell this story later, you make sure you let that part be known."

Fiona nodded. How the hell could she tell this story later?

"So Carr beat her, stabbed her and left her for dead in the compound. It was dumb luck that your dad found her. Saved her life. Kept her safe. She saw the picture in your office and… she's a wreck, Fi."

A wreck? *She* was a wreck? "It's a pretty big coincidence he ended up here." Coincidence her ass. Max and

Jez were big fat liars. Horrible liars who sacrificed a little boy so Jez could stay part of the club? The tarnish on her father's memory deepened in tone until it was nothing but a black blob. And Jez… goddammit.

"Not so much. She found him. She was waiting tables at some restaurant. And in walked this grungy kid with a scar on his head and a dimple in his chin. She said he looked just like she'd always imagined he would and she knew him right away. But some kids were giving him grief and he left before she ever got to talk to him. So she waited and waited for him to come back. When he told her his name, she knew for sure it was him. Then she told him about the club. Told Max about him. And the rest is… you know the rest."

Yeah. They'd both been manipulated into a marriage she'd thought was her choice.

Grier was the baby Jez gave away.

As far as Christmas gifts went, Grier had never really gotten into the whole Santa Claus, Night Before Christmas bullshit. Even last year, his first Christmas with Fiona, it had come and gone without much fanfare. He'd bought her a sweater. She'd bought him jeans and boots. But this year, his family had come to mean more than anything and holiday spirit Fa-la-la-la-la'ed through his blood.

He had Fiona's present tucked into his pocket and the baby's special "daddy" gift in a bag in the trunk. They had a few days yet and waiting to give the gifts might just kill him. He maneuvered into the driveway around the snow that had been plowed against the curb then climbed out.

The temps had gotten downright blustery and he hurried inside. "Honey… I'm home!" He called out like Ward Cleaver then stamped his boots against the rug Fiona had put in front of the door.

Fiona stumbled out of the kitchen. "Hey, baby." Her smile wavered even as she threw her arms around him and hugged him. He looked at Hamilton, asleep with his legs hanging over the arm of the sofa.

She moved back and he steadied her with a hand on each shoulder. "What's going on?"

Fiona shook her head, her mouth hanging open. "It's like Jerry Springer all up in here."

He didn't know what that meant, nor did he much care. Where the hell was London? "Where's the baby?"

"In her bed. Asleep. Like a little perfect angel." Fiona's head bobbed with every breath. "I just checked."

"And what's Hamilton doing here?" More he wanted to know why she was drunk, but he had a bad feeling the answer would ruin his good day.

"He's the messenger." She wagged a finger in front of Grier's face. "Don't shoot the messenger."

Goddammit. Fiona drunk in the middle of the day. What if he hadn't come home? What if something happened to the baby? She sure as hell couldn't take care of their kid, not like this. "I'm going to check on the baby. You need to go lie down and sleep it off."

She tilted her head and stared at him then nodded. "Yeah." And before he could speak, she turned and headed up the stairs.

Four hours later, Sage had come to get Hamilton, Grier had fed the baby from their reserve of pumped breast milk and cleaned the kitchen from her afternoon party with Hamilton. Fiona tromped down the stairs. She plopped on the couch next to him smelling as much like stale whiskey as she had earlier.

He didn't want to fight, but four hours of seething had spoiled any goodwill he had left. "I don't want you drinking when you should be watching our baby."

She nodded. "I know." She shook her head then closed her eyes and breathed out. "I'm sorry."

"What if something had happened?"

"I said I know, Grier. I'm sorry, and I won't do it again."

Well, that had to be good enough for now, didn't it? Except where he'd come from, promises meant shit. But this was Fiona. Not his foster mother. Not the woman who'd locked him in closets and… worse.

"Maybe you'd better tell me why." His voice was cold, too cold for him to feel good about the words.

"I will." She nodded. "But first, I need you to know I would never do anything… I don't… it was wrong and I'm so sorry." Her voice broke and she leaned forward to bury her head in her hands.

Had to be the hormones. The Fiona he knew didn't take orders except in the bedroom and she damned sure didn't cry over things she'd done but couldn't change.

He put an arm around her and hugged her. "Shh. It's okay."

After a few minutes of sobbing that shook her entire body, she lifted her head and dried her eyes leaving black smudges where she'd had rings of mascara before. "We have to talk."

That feeling in the pit of his stomach deepened to his bones. He forced it down and hardened his heart. If she was going to leave him or break him, he wouldn't fall apart. Not today. "All right."

But she stood and went to the kitchen, came back with a glass of water. The baby was awake and smiling at Grier as she held onto his finger and waved her arm around.

Fiona cleared her throat. "How'd you meet Jez?"

"She was a waitress in a diner downtown I used to go

to after school." And what the hell did that have to do with anything? But he knew it did. This wasn't Fiona's usual mode of small talk.

"So that's true." She nodded and ran the back of her finger over her lips. He'd seen her do it a thousand times. It was her thinking tell.

"Of course, it's true. Why would I lie about it?" He watched her. Her lips twitched from side to side.

"You wouldn't lie. You just don't, do you?"

"Not to you." His stomach churned. "Fiona, what is going on?" Meeting Jez had saved his life, started everything between him and Fiona, made him a Demon. Without Jez, he would've never met Max.

"Do you know what happened to your real parents? The woman who gave birth to you?"

He sighed. Obviously, until they played this stupid game of twenty-questions, she wasn't going to tell him whatever the hell happened to drive her to drink. "I don't know. And I don't care." Because of her, he'd been forced to endure unspeakable horrors, things he'd never even told her. "I was two or three when she threw me away and she never looked back so I never looked for her." He'd left the bitterness a long time ago, probably because he'd never talked about it before, but now, the taste of the words soured in his mouth.

"If you could meet her, would you?"

Maybe this had something to do with Fiona's

mother. He'd given her Max's letter a long time ago, assumed she'd read it, even though he hadn't, and also assumed that when Max had given it to him on his deathbed for Fiona, it would have her mother's name in it.

He twisted toward her, laying the baby across his lap. "No. I wouldn't. She gave up on me, and now that I have something good in my life, something precious and perfect," he smiled down at the baby then up at Fiona. "I don't need her. I did once. I prayed she would come back for me. Save me. I was just a little boy, but I prayed so hard. And she didn't come and it's too late now."

"Jez is your mom." No further preamble. No more questions. Just a blunt statement. Followed by, "And Willy Carr is your dad."

He stared at her until his mind transported him back to that day—the one where he'd met the kind waitress at Delucca's. Jez had been in her early thirties, tattooed, battle-scarred, and teary-eyed as Cameron Chancellor had taunted him. "Hey, Kermit. Where's Miss Piggy?" Then, he'd tried to trip Grier and when he stumbled, Cameron laughed and asked, "Kermit, can you tell me how to get, how to get to Sesame Street?" Loser had had it wrong. Kermit wasn't on Sesame Street, but Grier hadn't shared. It would only have made it worse.

At sixteen, almost seventeen, Grier was too small for Cameron to take him seriously. Already beaten by life.

Jez had "accidentally" poured a coffee in Cam's lap and he'd rushed out. Then she'd fed Grier his first meal outside of his school lunch in days.

"Bullshit."

"It's true." She told him the story while he sat ready with every new detail to puke his guts onto the floor.

He handed her the baby and went to the bedroom. Jez? The woman who abandoned him, then saved him. And goddamned if he knew what to do about it.

17

Fiona watched Grier. He slept peacefully with a smile on his face. He whistled while he showered. He ate breakfast with the gusto of a man who'd never seen food before. But then instead of getting dressed for the day, he lounged on the sofa in a pair of pajama pants with the baby and the remote clutched in his hand.

She moved to stand in front of the TV. "Grier?"

He lifted his gaze to her face. "Yeah?"

"Do we need to talk?" He raised his eyebrows and she couldn't read one damned thing. "About anything?"

His eyes hardened and his mouth compressed into a tight line. For one second then it all cleared away and he smiled. "No. I'm good. Do you need to talk about something?"

"What about yesterday?" She sputtered the words

because this was something she wanted him to *want* to talk to her about. But he only shrugged. Shrugged! "What about the club then? Aren't you going? There's a…" Madman? Who also happened to be his father. "Don't you want to talk to Jez?"

He stood and handed her the baby before walking into the kitchen and returning with a glass of orange juice. "Thought you wanted me to be Mr. Mom."

Who the hell was she turning into? She didn't need to talk about his feelings. Or hers. Max would spin in his grave if he knew she was standing in her house practically begging him to talk about his *feelings*. Dear God, when had she gone soft?

She nodded. "Yeah." And damned if she knew what the hell she was supposed to say or do. "Well, okay then."

Nothing to do now but get dressed and get to work. Back to her life.

Without her baby.

Knowing what she knew.

But she was Fiona Strong-Owen and she had courage no one even knew about. Intelligence. The ability to never show her hand.

And if that was true, she wouldn't have stood in the shower crying, torn between Jez and Grier. Not really torn, just a little ripped. Nothing she couldn't handle. And after today, no one would doubt her ability.

It took her all of twenty minutes to get ready. Today,

she wasn't Grier's wife or Max's daughter. She was Fiona, Leader of the Screaming Demons Motorcycle Club. And no one would question it. No one but Fiona, anyway.

She walked into the living room, took the baby, and almost teared-up at the thought of leaving her. Holding it back cost her a few deep breaths but she made it through. Grier smiled up at her from the sofa. "Hey, you have a good day." He winked and shot her a finger pistol.

No kiss. No hug. A fucking finger pistol.

"Yeah. You, too."

It didn't take a genius to know Grier wasn't doing so well with all the information she'd given him. Hell, she wasn't even sure how she was doing with it, and it didn't affect her more than heightening her curiosity about Jez.

She walked into her office to find Hamilton waiting in the chair across her desk. "God, it's good to see you back." He hugged her like she'd been across the country rather than across town and like he hadn't spent the afternoon yesterday drunk in her kitchen. She pulled back and walked around to sit in her chair. Hamilton stood, arms crossed, staring. "How did he take it?"

"He took it…" She shook her head. "I have no idea. He put up a wall so high I'm gonna need oxygen to clear that thing." Normally, she talked to Jez about things like this. Clearly, that was off the table now.

"He going to talk to her?"

Probably she shouldn't have been drunk when she told him. She would have been able to gauge his reaction, read him better, but too late. Without the assistance of Dr. Who or Marty McFly, she couldn't undo it. "I don't know. He didn't say."

"Are you going to talk to her?" Hamilton lowered his head. "Ask why she didn't mention how well she knew Carr?"

Now there was a suggestion she could get behind. They needed information and all the while, Jez had lived with this guy, known him. She nodded. "Yeah. Why don't you find her for me?" She needed a minute alone to sort this all out and watched Hamilton walk out.

Truth was, Fiona had so many questions she didn't know where to start and hadn't formulated a plan of attack yet when Jez closed the office door behind her. Hungover and without makeup, Jez looked older than her forty-four years. "Guess we all had too much to drink yesterday." Fiona smiled. She only knew she had to start off friendly, let Jez know… everything would be okay. Even though Fiona couldn't have said for certain.

"Yeah." Jez sat back in the chair but didn't speak for a few long seconds. "I guess he knows." She waited for Fiona's nod before she continued. "How is he?"

Honesty was all Fiona had. "I don't know. He seemed okay." She watched Jez, the slow nod, the way she bit the corner of her lower lip, the way she tried to hide the fact that she was breathing deep and letting it out. "Are you certain it's him? He's your… baby?"

"Yeah. He's the spitting image of my dad." She took off her necklace, a locket, opened it and handed it to Fiona. "Dad is on the left."

Fiona didn't have to ask who the baby on the right was. Instead, she concentrated on the man. Damned if Grier couldn't have been his twin. It took her a minute to hand the locket back. "Why didn't you just tell him?"

"I was scared." She shook her head and gripped the locket until her knuckles turned white. "A coward." When she glanced at Fiona her eyes were full of tears. "Your dad loved Grier. Even when he ran off, he would've never hurt him."

"And you loved Dad?" The answer didn't matter. Fiona knew the truth.

But Jez nodded. "He did everything he could for me back then and…" She dried her eyes with the butt of her hands and faced Fiona. "I loved him."

It didn't really explain why she'd lied to Grier, and Fiona couldn't decide if that was her business or not, so she moved on. "So what now?"

"Do you want me to leave?"

Fiona jerked her head back. Jez leave? She was as much a part of the Screaming Demons as Fiona herself. "God, no." Since Grier wouldn't talk about it, how the hell could Fiona know what he needed? No. Jez would stay. Grier would stay. And they would damned well figure out what to do. "This is personal business, not club business. I can't force you to stay any more than I could ever force you to leave. What happens now is between you and Grier."

"You're his wife."

How well she knew, even if he didn't seem to realize it right then. Until that moment, Fiona hadn't realized how his not talking to her about this hurt. But that was the last thing she wanted anyone to know. She smiled to cover whatever else Jez might have seen on her face. "And I guess that makes you my mother-in-law." She cocked her head. "You'll have to start calling before you come over so I can tidy up." Joking about it didn't help much, but until she spoke to Grier, it was all she had.

Jez smiled and looked down. "Did he… say anything?"

"No. He went to bed. Then he got up this morning and decided he wanted to be a stay at home dad today." And he'd probably be great at it because he was great at everything.

* * *

So FAR, the baby had turned into a vomit spewing devil. He'd been puked on, pissed on—the kid's bodily functions had gone haywire—and now, she wouldn't stop crying. His normally beautiful and well-dressed baby had gone rogue. The last thing he wanted to do was have to call Fiona home, but he didn't know what else to do. He'd walked and bounced, rocked, sang, turned on the TV, given her a bath—normally happy time in the house—and still… fat tears rolled down her cheeks.

The doorbell rang and he yanked it open. All he could hope was that Fiona had some motherly intuition and had sent in reinforcements to help him out. At this point, as confused and upset as he was, he would've welcomed Jez.

Instead Sage walked inside. "Wow." Of course, the place was a mess. The baby needed… stuff. And Grier could only manage to find the clothes, diapers, wipes, toys, blankets, but not so much to pick them up and put them away when they didn't work to calm the baby. Also, Grier didn't need Sage coming in laughing and judging.

"What are you doing here?"

Sage picked up a blanket, then the sleeper London had pissed on, then a diaper to toss at the trashcan. "Looks like I'm helping you." He held out his free arm. "Give me the kid."

"I'm not giving you my baby." Although he'd failed, so there wasn't much harm in letting Sage give it a try. "Seriously, what are you doing here?"

Sage continued picking up. "Where's the washing

machine?" Grier pointed and bounced the baby until Sage returned. "You have puke on your back." He circled Grier. "And in your hair." He held out his arm again. "Look, let me take her and you can get cleaned up. Then we need to talk about some club stuff."

"We can talk club stuff now." But unless he wanted the neighbors to hear everything, he'd have to find a way to quiet the baby so they didn't have to yell back and forth.

Sage looked him up and down. "I can't take you seriously while you're wearing enough baby puke to build another kid. Go shower."

Grier sighed. He could use the minute to calm himself. His entire life had been thrown into a backspin yesterday and maybe the baby could sense it because as soon as he handed her to Sage, she quieted. He looked down at her, so sweet and beautiful and, thank God, quiet now. "Fine."

And it annoyed him that Sage was right. He felt better after the shower, more ready to handle the baby at least. The rest of his life could wait.

He walked back into the living room. Sage sat on the sofa with a sandwich and London, feet on the coffee table, baby happy on his arm. "You better not have fed my kid any of that."

"Just a couple of bites of ham." He shrugged. "No big

deal." He handed Grier the baby and shoveled the last bite of his sandwich into his face.

"Club business?"

Sage held up one finger while he chewed then swallowed. "Word on the street is that some of the Midtown Thugs got roughed up last night."

Grier shrugged. "So?"

"Street also says that it was some group called the Omens."

Again, so? "Who are the Omens?"

"Another club." He nodded. "Tyler Sedotal's club."

Okay. Now Sage had his attention. "Does Fiona know?"

Sage sighed. "I'm not done." Sage laid the story out. The Omens wanted some help from the Thugs who declined because "they don't kill babies".

"I have to call Fiona." He dialed and waited for her to answer. "Can you come home? We have to talk."

The panic in her voice rang through his head. "Is it the baby? Is something wrong?"

"No, she's fine. I just need..." He sighed. "Can you come home?" And because he needed her to take it seriously, he added, "Please?"

"I'll be right there."

He probably should've told her not to rush or take any crazy chances with red lights, but he needed her here with him. Where he could protect his family.

"Good." He hung up before he blurted out the whole thing. He needed to get the rest of the details out of Sage and couldn't wait for Fiona. "Tell me all of it."

"Tyler Sedotal has something planned. And at least a part of it is about your wife and your baby. And I say it that way because this doesn't seem to be about the club, but about you personally."

And for the first time, it occurred to him that if Willy Carr was his father, Tyler Sedotal was his brother. "Son of a bitch." Now he just had to figure out why his... brother... and maybe his father wanted him and his family dead.

iona stared at Grier. This was crazy. "How reliable is your intel?" It could have been a set-up, or a hoax or... but Grier believed it enough to call her home, to not let go of the baby.

Sage stared at her, his arms folded, his stance wide. "I feel like it's pretty credible. What reason do they have to lie to me?"

Fiona could think of thousands of reasons and most of them had pictures of dead presidents on them. "I don't know, Sage, but to go after a baby? That's..." It was pretty far-fetched. No Demon would even consider hurting a baby.

"They didn't go after London. They called me."

"Not me, the target, or Grier." That said a lot in her mind. But Grier laid his free hand on her shoulder and she turned to look at him. Actual fear glittered in his eyes.

"Fiona, I think we have to take this seriously until we know it isn't." He looked down at the baby. "You and London are all I have." That wasn't quite true since he had every guy at the club, Jez, even if he didn't want her, and apparently enough respect from other clubs they'd called in their warning. But since he looked so damned already, and desperate, she let him go on. "Please, let's just get you out of here until I can, at least, neutralize this threat."

Normally, she would've never agreed. Never even considered. But a threat to her baby, even if it wasn't real, along with the look on Grier's face made her protest more token, less protest. "What's it say to them, to the Demons even, if I run and hide?"

"I don't give a fuck what it says to anybody. I need to know my wife and my baby are safe. Jesus, Fiona… please, just do this one thing without a fight, without knowing more than me. Just this once." His words weren't as bitter as they were fraught with emotion. Husky. Deep. A plea.

"I can protect myself."

"Yeah. I have no doubt, but this is not just about you or me. It's about London. Are you really going to let your pride risk her life?"

Low blow, but she nodded. Better to give in now and

try to figure out a way to stay later. "All right." But nothing about it felt good, nothing about picking up her shit and running away made her happy. "I'll go." She even managed a smile when Grier leaned in to press his lips against her forehead. "Are you coming with us?"

They could call it a vacation.

"No. I can't. You know I can't." He spoke softly but the message came through loud and clear. Her leaving was one thing, but she knew he would never leave as long as Tyler Sedotal was out there making his threats and causing havoc for the club.

As they continued to talk, any tenderness faded from Grier's eyes only to be replaced by a ferocity that broadened his shoulders, made him taller and more dangerous than Fiona could remember. "I could ask Kye." He didn't see Fiona's rolled eyes because he hadn't looked at her in a while.

"Really? I threatened him, might have even killed him had I not gone into labor. That almost killed me." She hadn't used that card yet, but if refreshing his memory of how she'd almost died to have his baby made him reconsider sending her to some godforsaken island with a man she didn't trust and a woman who'd almost cost the club everything, then by God, it was her card to play. "Do you really think he's the best choice for bodyguard?"

"I do." Grier nodded. "I can't be there. And I need

Sage and Ham here." He finally turned to her. "Fiona, I love you and I would never do anything I thought would put you in danger. Ever. Kye will protect you because he's... my family, and you and London are my family. And that means something to him."

And if Kye failed, Fiona would protect her baby. It didn't matter where she was. "Okay."

He smiled. "You can work on your tan."

She narrowed her eyes. "Redheads don't tan. We freckle." And now she'd have to buy big hats, but for Grier, she would. At least if she couldn't convince him to at least send her somewhere else.

GRIER CUDDLED FIONA CLOSER. She hadn't mentioned leaving since they'd talked with Sage, but with Fiona, silence was never really silence. More a calm before the storm. And judging by how long she'd kept quiet, this was probably going to be a funnel cloud of anger.

But if it had to be, to keep her safe, he'd weather it.

After another hour of lying silently in the dark, she squirmed out of his arms and turned to flip on the bedside lamp. "I've been shooting guns since I was old enough to hold one. I could probably protect myself and London. And you would be here. We would be together."

Though she spoke rationally, anyone who knew her knew she could turn on a dime.

And Grier sure as hell wasn't dumb enough to argue that particular point. Fiona could probably shoot straighter than he did. "I know, but if something happened to you or the baby…" His throat closed and words failed him. He shook his head hoping she understood how hard this was for him.

"We could have Ham stay with us."

Not that he hadn't considered it. Hamilton was a lot of man, but even someone his size couldn't stand up against a shotgun shell or an AK. And Fiona knew it. "I need to know that you're safe so I can get this fucker and put an end to all of this." They wouldn't be safe until Sedotal was out of their lives.

She narrowed her eyes. "So since you and Sage are deciding everything now, did you decide when I'm leaving?"

And here it was—the first of the storm clouds. "As soon as we can get a plane lined up with a flight plan."

"So I should just pack and sit and wait for you to give me my orders?" She turned away. "Great."

"There's nothing I can do that makes more sense than this." He didn't want his wife and baby so far away, where he couldn't wake up in the morning and kiss Fiona or breathe in the sweet smell of London's hair. No. He wanted them with him, every minute of every day, but he couldn't be two places at one time. It simply wasn't possible and there was no one in the world he trusted more than Kye to keep his family safe. "I know you're mad at me. And I hate it, but I love you so much, and I can't risk losing you because I left you unprotected."

Loving her the way he did actually caused a physical ache in his guts when he thought of losing her. And if telling her made him less of a man, then so be it.

He wanted to hold her, to absorb her, not fight. Not argue. Especially over this. Or anything else that happened in the last few days. It was all too much and this was the thing he needed to worry about right now. Everything else would wait.

She huffed out a breath then spun around to flip off her light. Then she yanked the blanket to her side of the bed and formed a tight cocoon around herself. And damned if he would let her go to sleep mad at him on what was probably going to be their last night together for a while.

He scooted to her side and pulled the blanket down to kiss her shoulder. She didn't jerk backward and bust him in the mouth, so he took it as a good sign and moved his mouth to her throat while his hand snaked under the blanket.

When he got to her ear, he whispered, "I love you."

He ran his fingers across her belly then lower, to tease her thighs apart. "Let me touch you."

She sighed soft and low. Not frustrated. Willing.

He closed his eyes to savor the moment she turned to face him. Her lips feathered over his jaw as she wrapped an arm around his neck. "I love you, Grier."

If he died right then, with a hard dick and balls so tight they were on the verge of explosion, he would never be happier. This was his wife, the one woman who he would never be able to live without and tonight, he planned to show her just how much she meant to him.

When he slipped inside her, he watched her, the wideness of her eyes, the softness in her smile. She clung to him, holding him inside her with her arms and legs. "Don't ever stop loving me."

Every part of Grier was wrapped up in Fiona, but hearing her words, knowing she loved him despite all the stuff they were going through, made his heart soar. Tonight wasn't about their playfulness or their marriage. It was about the way they felt about each other and showing it.

He moved slow, touched her face, kissed her with such tenderness, and it was as erotic as having her obey his bedroom commands. She arched against him, dragged her mouth across his throat, and made that lovely whimpering sound that always meant she was close. And her being close brought him to the edge.

"Fiona!" His cry landed in her hair as he rocked forward and she met him with a cry of her own.

And oh Lord, he was on the verge of tears. Nothing in his life had meant more to him than this night, her holding him, asking him to never stop loving him. And no matter what he did, for the rest of his life, he would earn the love she'd given back.

* * *

HE HELD her through the night and woke to her stroking his cock. For a shameful minute, he considered that she might be using sex to try to convince him to let her and the baby stay, but by the time he had the thought, she added her mouth into the mix and further thought wasn't possible.

Oh, God. This woman. She had magic in her. And she sat up, naked and glorious over him, and lowered herself onto him. He watched her. Such passion on her face, such emotion and ecstasy. He didn't deserve so much, but damned if he would ever let her go.

When he moved his hips in time with hers, she used her legs to press him against the bed. "Let me."

And it took all his concentration, all his strength to remain still and let her be in charge, and he did until the frenzy took over and he couldn't just lie there anymore. He sat up and held her, rising and falling with her. Every time with Fiona was exciting, but today meant more which made it feel more... of everything.

When they finished, even after their bodies quit moving, she straddled his lap with her arms around his neck and her head buried in his shoulder. "I'm going to miss you." She sniffed softly.

"Are you crying?"

She sat back far enough to see his face. The tears there almost killed him. "Of course I'm crying, you big ass. What if... something happens? And what if..."

He smoothed her hair. "Shh. Nothing bad is going to happen and you're going to be back here as soon as possible. Maybe I'll even come and get you. We can leave London with Kye for an hour or so and make love in the ocean." And on the beach, and under the stars, in the rain, on a sunny afternoon.

Fiona cocked an eyebrow. "Is sex all you ever think about?"

There she was. His wife. "You're sitting on me naked. What else would I be thinking about?"

She curled her fingers into his hair and pulled him in for a kiss that was neither gentle nor sweet, but hot as hell. "Well, maybe you should stop thinking about it and just... do it."

So, he did.

19

Sage loaded Fiona's bags into Jez's car while Fiona stood in the living room watching Grier strap the baby into her car seat. If anything happened to him… she'd battled the lump in her throat all morning. Well, since she finally let him out of bed, anyway. She left her spot against the wall and put a hand on his shoulder.

He stood and wrapped her in a hug and she breathed him in, the scent of the soap she bought for him, the conditioner she'd rubbed through his hair, the scent of his skin that was simply Grier. God. She didn't want to go. She would rather stay there and face death, but he was right. Their baby was more important than her pride at being sent away.

She stared at Grier. Aside from his incredible beauty, there was a strength and a tenderness that she would never have expected. And God help her, everything she noticed made her love him more, need him in ways she couldn't have imagined were real.

"I'll come and get you. I promise you. As soon as I know you're safe here."

And she believed him. "I knew I should have just dragged you to Mayberry."

He leaned his forehead against hers. "We'll find our Mayberry." His gaze searched her face. "Who knows? You might even like it so much there, you don't want to come back."

"Is that how it was for you?" She didn't want to go on that note, but she had to know.

"You, silly girl. I came back for you. It's always been you. And it's always going to be you." He kissed her softly, so softly she wanted more but didn't want to change the moment into something else. Instead, she laid her head over his chest and listened, etching the sound into her memory.

"Don't stop loving me."

He hugged her tighter. "I couldn't if I tried."

"And don't forget me."

He grinned. "I have video." His breath ruffled her hair. "Kye knows what to do if you need me. And he knows when I'll call so he'll take you to the place, okay?"

Fiona nodded, for all the world feeling like she was

losing him. "Just get this done quickly so we can come home."

Finally she pulled away when Sage picked up the baby's chair. Grier kissed Fiona one last time and walked her out to the car where he kissed her again. "Soon, I promise."

She nodded as Sage pulled the car away from the curb. She'd seen a hundred movies where the heroine and hero were being taken away from each other for one reason or another and the heroine always put her hand on the window in one of those sappy moves designed to tug at the viewers' heartstrings. After today, Fiona didn't think it was sappy anymore.

* * *

WOAH. When Sage booked a plane, he booked a plane—a five-seater, and by seat, she meant luxury leather captain's chair seats with padding so plush it felt like feathers enveloping her body, a built-in footrest, and a headrest softer than her pillow at home. Max would've loved this thing. And Fiona was quite convinced this was the only way to fly. Wow.

When no stewardess greeted her, she buckled the baby's car seat into the one next to her and braced herself for what was about to happen, the upward climb at take-off that made her stomach dance inside of her, and not in the good way, the ear-popping when the plane leveled, the feeling of everything dropping out as the plane tilted down for landing. And that would only get her as far as refueling. Then she'd have to go through it all again.

She'd made this flight once, not so luxuriously, but she knew they would arrive in something like six and a half hours, so she'd brought a book, and snacks, and she'd stuffed the diaper bag full of things she could use to quiet the baby. Even the white noise machine she kept plugged by the crib.

And she'd checked and rechecked the weather, probably a hundred times that morning, to make sure they wouldn't be traveling into a storm or bad weather. This would be a smooth flight. She repeated the words to herself, once, twice, fifty times as she sat waiting for the pilot to start the plane.

Finally, the engine roared to life outside the window. She watched the turbine turn and breathed out.

* * *

GRIER HADN'T BEEN able to stay away. He'd tried, wanted to, but he stood at the airport watching the small plane taxi down the runway then lift off, taking his wife and daughter to safety.

When he couldn't see the plane anymore, he turned away from the window and walked through the airport.

"I knew you'd be here." Sage stood and put the newspaper he'd been reading down. "Plus, I saw you following us on your bike. You're horrible at surveillance."

Grier nodded. "I couldn't decide between stopping you and just following." He'd considered chasing down the car and telling Fiona to stay. But talked himself out of it. He shrugged.

"She's safe now. And you can concentrate on finding Sedotal and putting that fucker down."

For no other reason would he have let Fiona go. "Yeah."

They took a couple of steps toward the door before Sage said, "And you can talk to Jez."

Grier shook his head. "Leave that alone, okay? It's not something I can think about right now."

"I'm just saying—"

"Yeah, well, don't." He snapped the words. This was his business. It had nothing to do with anyone at the club except him and Jez and until he decided how to handle it, he intended to forget it.

Right now, he had to figure out why his brother— and if anything in the world felt odder to say, he couldn't think of what it would be—and his brother's gang wanted to hurt Fiona and London. If it was about hurting Grier, he could accomplish that easily enough. But why? This went deeper than club rivalry. This was personal since he wasn't going after the club, but after Grier's family.

"I think we need to know what Sedotal's after."

"You, obviously."

"Yeah, but why? What does he hope to accomplish by taking me out? I don't run the club. I mean I did while Fiona was out with the baby, but not when this all started with the missing shipments and the…" His heart ached as he remembered. "The explosion. It might have been about the club then but now… Fiona and the baby…"

Sage nodded. "I was thinking about that. Do you have some sort of connection between you two? A reason he would go after you?"

Telling everyone about his connection to Sedotal would open Grier to more suspicion. Make them question his return and the timing with which the shitstorm started, probably make them think he was in on it and that he'd sent Fiona away because she was either his accomplice—God he hoped no one would believe that about her—or to get her out of his way while he took the club down out of some ridiculous familial obligation.

And there it was. The reason Sedotal had chosen now to act. Son of a bitch. He'd figured it out. Of course, he had no one he could tell it to. He'd just put the only person who believed in him completely on a plane to Belize.

* * *

GRIER WALKED into the clubhouse and sat at the bar. Nothing like having it all in his face, all the time. Autumn handed him a beer. "Where's Jez?"

Autumn shrugged. "Not my day to keep track." She walked to the other end of the bar and smiled at Hamilton. Hamilton smiled back, as much as Hamilton ever smiled, anyway, and Sage sat beside Grier.

"So what's the plan?"

He didn't have one. "Kind of hoping you had one."

Sage twisted his chair and leaned back against the bar, his elbow dangerously close to Grier's bottle. And with nothing else to do but sit there and think and drink, Grier took a long pull from his beer.

"We need to figure out the end game and work our way backward." As if Grier wouldn't understand his thinking, he continued. "You know, what's he getting in the end?" To hurt Grier was the obvious answer. Obvious to Grier, anyway. But Sage went on. "Wouldn't be the club. These guys are loyal as hell to Fiona… and to you as long as you're married to her." He bobbed his head from one side to the other. "So, that's good and bad. If he kills her, there'll be moves against you. But why would he keep her alive otherwise?" Grier glared and Sage held up his hands. "Sorry. Just spitballing here. What if it's about our, um… clientele? He wants the business Fiona controls." Sage nodded, his smile pleased. "Yeah. That's gotta be it. He wants her for the business."

"Maybe."

Sage turned back to the bar, signaled for a beer from Amber then turned to Grier. "No, it has to be. And he was going to take your baby to make her give him the information."

It was plausible. Reasonable, even if Sedotal turned out to be the brother Grier had never had. "Yeah."

"Although the Thug didn't say 'take the baby'. He said, 'kill the baby'. And Fiona would bleed him if he hurt your kid." Sage drilled his fingers on the bar. "Shit."

Grier sighed. "Jez is my mom."

Sage nodded. "I know. She mentioned it."

"Willy Carr is my dad." The rest, Carr being Tyler Sedotal's father, was common knowledge.

It took a couple of seconds but Sage's eyes widened and his mouth dropped open. "Sedotal is your brother?" When Grier nodded, Sage puffed his cheeks and blew out slowly. "Holy shit."

Grier nodded. "Yeah. That was pretty much how it hit me, too. Except my drunk wife told me."

Sage whistled under his breath. "No wonder."

Not that he really cared, but it was a conversation. He probably needed to take some part in it lest it lose its status. "No wonder what?"

"The way she watches you. Jez, not Fiona. I mean Fiona watches you, but different. She undresses you with her eyes."

And just like that, Grier missed his wife even more. "Seriously. Move on."

"Jez watches you like she wants to follow you around and make sure you don't scratch up your knees or bump your head. Like a mom would watch her kid." He shrugged. "But lately, since this shit started, she's been a wreck. Door opens, she's reaching for her gun. She knows you're in danger."

And never said anything? "Where's she at?"

"I haven't seen her all day."

Jez had her own house, but she spent more time behind the bar at the club than the total of the guys spent on the other side. "Come on." Grier hopped off the stool and stood. "Hey, Hamilton." When Hamilton looked up, Grier waved him over. "Come on. We have to go. Now."

If not the wife, the mother? Fuck.

20

The wheels made that slick hard brake sound as it touched down and Fiona looked out of the window. Woah. This was one small airport they'd landed at. She admired Sage's planning. Quite the little mastermind, not flying her into a commercial airport where… where she would be surrounded by security personnel, the ATF, probably ICE agents, cops, people in general.

She looked out of the window again. This was a hangar in the middle of a group of fields. She reached for her cell and remembered that Grier had made her leave it in Pine Hill. She pulled the inflight phone from the wall that connected her to the cockpit.

"Sit back and relax for a few minutes, Mrs. Owen, and we'll get you situated."

They'd been in the air less than three hours. And

what the actual fuck did he mean by situated? She unbuckled her seat belt and stood, saw a pair of ugly blue pumps in the rear of the plane. The fact they were attached to a pair of legs prone and motionless made Fiona's breaths come fast and hard, a pant.

"What's going on?" Her demand into the receiver was met by silence, but the cockpit door opened and a man dressed, not as a pilot but as a biker, complete with leather and a gun in a hip holster, walked out and down the aisle. He was older, beaten by the years, but she would have guessed him about fifty maybe a little older, but their lifestyle didn't age men well.

And with danger imminent, she didn't have time to consider his looks for another second. She fell back into her seat, putting her body between this asshole and her baby. He really would have to kill her to get to London. "Who the fuck are you?"

"Oh don't worry, beautiful. We're gonna get to know each other really well. Now. You do as I say, and you and your little bundle of joy get to walk off the plane. You try me, and you're walking off alone because I'm going to shoot her, right in her pretty little face." When Fiona didn't move, he pulled the pistol from its spot and aimed it at London.

Fiona held up her hand. "All right. All right. I'm going."

She unlatched the seat, lifted the carrier and slipped the diaper bag over her shoulder.

"Here, let me help you." He reached for the carrier and because of the tight quarters, all Fiona could do was hold on as tight as she had the strength for.

"I can manage." Fiona's stomach turned on his smile.

"I'm afraid I have to insist." He jerked the carrier and Fiona gasped.

"Please don't hurt her. I'll do whatever you want. Whatever you say." And when this was over, she would blow this son of a bitch into a thousand pieces.

He nodded. "I know. Now come on. There's someone who's just dying to meet the two of you."

Her list started with Tyler Sedotal. And whoever this fucker was. But by the time this was over, she was willing to bet it would be full of names of people she was going to kill. Slowly.

* * *

Grier and Hamilton flew toward Jez's little house in Hull with Sage not far behind. He had to get there, make sure she was safe and sound.

He pulled up next to Hamilton in front of the house. All the lights were on… in every room and the door was closed. He couldn't see any sign of distress or confrontation, so he climbed off his bike and stepped onto the sidewalk. The sun was low in the sky, which meant little since it was December, but Grier knew daylight wasn't on their side. He waited for Sage to pull up. "Ham, take the back. I'm going front and Sage, you watch the street. Nothing gets past. All right?"

Sage nodded and pulled a shiny Glock from his back.

He parked the bike and climbed off then went to stand in the shadow of a tree from where he could see the house and street equally. Grier pulled the gun he kept in the saddle bag of his bike and went to the door. His knock was met with silence. "Jez, if you're home, answer the door."

Nothing. Silence.

"Jez. Come on." He knocked again. "Open the door or I'm coming in." He tried the knob. Locked. "Last chance, Jez."

He banged with his fist now and when he didn't get an answer, he put his shoulder against wood and slammed his way through. The house was trashed, her furniture shredded, lamps upturned, TV smashed. "Fuck!"

Hamilton burst through the back and Sage stood in the doorway. Grier checked the bedroom, the kitchen, and the bathroom. All equally trashed, and no sign of Jez.

"She's not here."

"You think he has her?" Sage slid his gun into his

waistband and walked further into the room to pick up a picture of Jez, younger and holding a baby. He handed it to Grier.

Hamilton turned a pasty shade of green then ran out of the back door.

"Well, she sure as hell didn't do this to her own house."

But at least Fiona was safe. That was all that mattered. That and finding his mother.

DARK DESIRES

~ A billionaire dark romance series ~

Dark Desire

Dark Rules

Dark Secret

Dark Time

Dark Truth

BARRE TO BAR

~ A billionaire second chance series ~

Dancing With Lies

Dancing With Temptation

Dancing With Doubt

Dancing With Guilt

Dancing With Redemption

TWISTED INTENTION
~ A billionaire revenge romance series ~
Twisted Beauty
Twisted Love
Twisted Fate

Mafia's Obsession
~ A hot mafia romance series ~
Mafia's Dirty Secret
Mafia's Fake Bride
Mafia's Final Play

Screaming Demons
~ An MC romance series full of suspense ~
Rough Start
Rough Ride
Rough Choice
Rough Patch
Rough Return
Rough Road
Rough Trip
Rough Night
Rough Love

Standalone Contemporary Romance
Billionaire in Vegas
Billionaire Hunt

Billionaire's Game

Billionaire Retreat

Billionaire On Air

A Chance To Love

Somebody To Love

Not Mine To Love

Check out Summer's entire collection at
www.summercooper.com/books

ABOUT SUMMER COOPER

Thank you so much for reading. Without you, it wouldn't be possible for me to be a full-time author. I hope you enjoy reading my books as much as I do writing them.

Besides (obviously!) reading and writing, I also love cuddling my dogs, shouting at Alexa, being upside down (aka Yoga) and driving my family cray-cray!

Get in touch at
hello@summercooper.com
www.summercooper.com

facebook.com/summercooperauthor
instagram.com/summercooperauthor
goodreads.com/summercooper
bookbub.com/profile/summer-cooper